For Julie,
I hope you enjoy
the magic and mystery.

Andrea

The Curious Ways of the Winships

By Andrea Mina Savar

This book is dedicated to my Grandparents and all my family who have gone before them.

"In nature, nothing is created, nothing is destroyed, everything is transformed." –Antoine Lavoisier

CHAPTER 1

It was a curious beginning to the season when autumn came in a fiery flash of brilliant red leaves overnight. Seattle had been experiencing an unusual amount of blue skies and green leaves until, on the ides of October, every single leaf blazed vermillion. It was at this moment that I, Charlotte Winship, had the overwhelming sensation that death would soon take someone close to me. The nagging darkness hovered in the corners all that morning. I tried to brush it aside as I opened all the windows to let in the suddenly crisp air. But nothing could erase the feeling of grief that came along with the violent red reflections of the trees outside. Of one thing I was sure: death would come. After all, it is the one thing in the world that is unfailingly nonnegotiable.

It wasn't only the looming darkness that had me fidgeting my way through the morning. I also felt an intense sense of dread at the thought of being pulled back to my childhood home. I had left my birthplace of Port Townsend, Washington three years earlier in the hopes of creating a new life for myself where no one had heard of my family and their strange gifts. Until the day of the red leaves, all had been going well with my plan of anonymity. I lived in a small house with my boyfriend James. I had a jewelry studio where I created gemstone adornments for local stores and I had a nice group of ordinary friends who had no inkling of my unique vision of the world. The ghosts of my youth had been neatly tucked away into the attic where no one in my new life would bother to snoop. Then the inexplicable notion that promised a coming disaster invaded my perfectly normal new life.

As the day wore on the darkness had me to near panic. It was inching its way closer as the orange sunset tore a gash across the Seattle skyline. By the time I crawled into bed next to James my heart was pounding so loudly, I was sure that it would wake him. Instead I somehow fell into a deep sleep. That was when the dream came on black-feathered wings. It rushed through an open window, stealing into the house the moment that I had drifted to where the veil between worlds was thin. A dark angel was in the room with me. It was whispering secrets into my ear of destruction and turmoil. It was telling me to go home.

My eyes shot open and I felt a surge of adrenaline flood my body as I lay frozen under the warm blankets. I could hear James' melodic breathing next to me, as it was the only sound that filled the perfect still of our silent bedroom. I glanced at the bedside clock to see the glow of neon numbers reading 3:00 am. Lifting myself out of the warmth of our bed, I swiftly made my way to the living room. Tiptoeing down the dark hall, I tried to reach the kitchen as quickly as possible. In my gut I knew that the phone was about to ring. My hand hovered over the receiver anticipating the call so as not to alarm James. If my intuition was right, I would be making the ferry ride and hour drive back to Port Townsend in the dawn hours as soon as I got the confirming phone call announcing tragedy. I could still feel the cold sweat from the dream chilling me and a pulling sensation like a thread attached to my navel calling me home. The house cracked as it settled into the autumn night, leaving me to shiver in the darkness waiting to hear my mother's voice on the other line.

I knew eventually I would have to return home. It was as if the tides were always pulling at me, insisting that I was meant to live in that one odd little corner of the world. Situated on the tip of the Olympic Peninsula with only the cold Pacific Ocean straights separating it from Canada, Port Townsend was originally slated to be a major US port when it was officially founded in 1851. Initially people had called it the 'city of dreams' with lofty visions of a prosperous future. The town was dressed up in all its finery waiting for a party that simply never arrived as the great depression hit and the Pacific Railroad stopped construction in Seattle. From that moment on Port Townsend became a ghost town in many senses of the word. The ornate Victorian homes were lived in and passed from one generation to the next like hand-me-down clothes. The downtown area was boarded up with the exception of the town saloons where bootleggers hid barrels of liquor in the old Shanghai trap doors as the locals drank away their worries along with their hopes and dreams.

If it hadn't been for the sudden influx of wealthy residents in the 1970s the town would surely have disintegrated into piles of termite ridden dust. Even with the new determination to make the town a landmark, the long years of isolation had left a town turned in on itself where locals are weary of newcomers and tourists are seen as both a blessing and a curse. Most of the tourists that visit the town of Port Townsend during the sunny summers are there for the wooden boat festival and have not the slightest notion that so many haunts are watching over them. But if you drive into town on a rainy winter day after a storm has just rolled through the atmosphere is quite different. The charming facades of the downtown buildings suddenly look darker and if the light hits the upper windows right, you may see a shadow or a face looking back at you from an empty room. The bell tower high on the cliff over-looking the water occasionally rings of its own accord calling ghostly firemen to put out a long forgotten flame and the empty streets in the dark winter nights are empty of locals for a reason.

But of all the strange things that make up Port Townsend, the locals would almost all agree that my family, the Winships, are the strangest of them all. It all started long before I was born with a lineage of women who could see things others couldn't and control the elements in ways that were beyond explanation. Though we were far from the days of burning witches the regular townsfolk had a healthy respect for any woman with the name Winship. I am the last female in the line of raven-haired women and while my family had many sweet nicknames for me growing up the whispered name around town that everyone else called me behind my back was 'Graves'. This was so for two reasons: the first was because I spent an inordinate amount of time with my grandfather cleaning the graveyard grounds. The second reason was that most people in town knew that I had a peculiar way of communicating with the lingering dead. To say this unnerved people would be an understatement.

My grandmother, Margot Winship, was generally referred to as formidable by all who knew her and would not have tolerated a town nickname, but my mother and I hadn't fared as well. It was a well-known fact in town that Winship women always kept their family name even in the days when it was socially unacceptable. Only once did a local official try to challenge the rule during my great-grandmother Elsiba's wedding, but the searing pain that shot through his chest and down his left arm quickly ended any more dispute in the matter. So wherever there was a Winship, she usually came with a nickname, as she tended to stand out in such a small town.

My mother, Deidre Winship, was called the 'Magpie' because birds of all sorts flocked to her with their secrets. Loose strands of her long black hair could be found in their winter nests all over town. They brought her gifts and built their roosts above her bedroom window. I'm sure that some people in town even imagined that she could fly. My family inspired all sorts of fantastical ideas in a population desperate to escape the mundane tasks of daily life. And while many were not far from the truth, we were still bound to the usual limitations of the human body.

The rustle of dark angel wings that had slipped into my room tonight reminded me of one of her birds. This carrion messenger had spoken of a treasure plucked from inside the old Winship house. It was tucked in its beak like a writhing worm and as it flew out the open window a man's voice screamed my name. Still waiting by the phone I could hear the ticking of the nearby clock and my bare legs began to tremble with cold. The increasingly ominous feeling in the pit of my stomach began to rise like bile into my mouth. As the first ring sounded through the silence, I frantically answered feeling both terrified and relieved to hear my mother's familiar voice.

"Mom, what is it? Who died? Is it Margot?" I asked, dreading the answer. I could hear the old bell tower's long retired bell ringing in the background, which confirmed that something very out of the ordinary had happened. The town ghosts would only sound the bell when imminent danger was about to strike Port Townsend.

"Come home Charlotte, it has to do with your Uncle," Deidre's voice sounded strangely cold on the other line as she tried to explain, 'there has been an accident and it seems that we are having a funeral on Friday.'

"I'll leave as soon as James is awake," I assured her as my voice started to tremble with shock, "I should be able to make the first ferry." I could feel her nod on the other end of the line and then heard the dial tone. It was her none too subtle way of telling me that the rest would be revealed when I was back in her territory and there was no way for me to run away.

A million thoughts raced through my mind, my Uncle Morgan had been missing for over three years. Her vague words implied that there was much more to what was going on than just a simple accident. Morgan Winship was my mother Deidre's twin brother. And while she was born with her bird guardians and kind nature, her brother was her exact opposite. If there was trouble to be found one could be sure that Morgan would be knee deep in it with his quick mind and quicker tongue.

Not knowing what else to do I started a pot of coffee in the hopes that I could wile at least another two hours away until I could make my way across the Puget Sound on the first ferry. I could feel the adrenaline beginning to wane and a sense of anxiety building in its place as I began to think back on that last time I had seen Uncle Morgan. The male Winships were always rare and generally considered forces of nature both good and bad. There hadn't been a male born in the family for over one hundred years and a twin was never considered a good omen, especially one born breach like Uncle Morgan. Deidre had been born at 3:00 am emerging into the world and Margot's arms with a smile on her face and an instant aura of calm. Morgan, however, had followed feet first nearly ending Margot's young life. She had struggled for hours in agony to bring forth a child that was marked with a star on his right shoulder and a temperament that would later cause devastation not only to the Winship house, but to the town at large.

Sitting at the kitchen table listening to the coffee pot gargle out a familiar tune, the memory of my last visit with Uncle Morgan began to stir. Wherever he went fire was usually bound to follow and whether he simply attracted it or caused it no one really knew. The last time I saw him he was running out of a blazing house. He disappeared that very day leaving us behind to clean up the soot and the ashes all the time wondering what had become of him. For days after Margot's sorrow at the disappearance of her only son brought on violent storms to the coast. As she cried with more intensity, it seemed that the rain followed suit and the waves that came crashing onto the shores of the Peninsula were unforgiving in their destruction. By the end of that October week the bridge that connected the town to the mainland had been washed away to sea and Port Townsend would suffer in its isolation, as it once again became a ghost town.

I had left soon after with no prospects of making a living as a young jewelry designer in a town that would soon have no tourists because of the missing link to the mainland and only one ferry boat every few days. Uncle Morgan's disappearance had plunged Margot into a deep melancholy and when I told her that I too was leaving I feared it might be the end of her. I was therefore shocked when she gave me her stash of mad money to get myself started in the city and a small lockbox with very specific items for protection, fortune and love. My mother Deidre had not been as open to the idea of my leaving as I was only 19 and had a rather strange way of seeing the world. She worried that the city would overwhelm me just to swallow me whole. But in the end she sent me away with good luck wishes and a little robin that followed me everywhere for the first few weeks.

A series of groans sounded from the bedroom as James' alarm went off and I heard the shower turn on. I was brought back to the moment as I finished my second cup of coffee. The realization finally set in that I would be heading back to Port Townsend after nearly three years of being absent from that strange little town with all its expectations of me. I made my way into our bedroom and switching on the light I saw my own reflection in the upright mirror near my dresser. Long black hair, petite, pale skin and dark eyes, I looked like any other twenty-two year old city girl as I put on my favorite jeans with the rip in the knee, a black t-shirt and a grey sweater with a hood. Here in Seattle I knew how to blend. But while I started to pack a few things for my return home, including my favorite black dress, I couldn't help but cringe at how appropriate all the town folk would think it was that 'Graves' was coming home again for a funeral.

CHAPTER 2

I could see the ferry pulling into the dock right at 6am on schedule. I sat in my car with the motor off dreading the trip ahead for various reasons. James had been supportive as always and offered to take a few days off and come with me but the thought of him being with my family on their turf during turmoil was too much for me to juggle. Instead of flat out telling him "No," I did a bit of diplomatic dissuading so as not to hurt his feelings and convinced him I would be home quickly. Deep down I knew that I needed just to be myself with them and there was still too much that James didn't know about the Winships and most of all about me. He knew the basics of my childhood but the whole point of my getting out of Port Townsend was to leave my ghosts behind.

James was as normal as they come. He had no special abilities beyond his above average intelligence, unless a good sense of humor counts and he adored me without my having to use any Winship charms or tricks to catch a man's attentions. There had been no need for subtle spells or specially bound amulets left under his doorstep -- not that I had ever used any of these methods; it had all happened naturally. But I still felt that it was too soon to let him in on all there was to know about me, the odd girl from the sleepy-hollow town. I am sure he had his suspicions when I knew who was calling before the phone rang or when I would hum the music he had listened to on the way home from work as he walked in the door. But he knew better than to push me about anything. So when I started my engine and rolled onto the docked ferry alone, I knew that it was time to let my guard down and make my way back home.

The boat was only half-full as it pulled out into the straights. Monday morning in the middle of October was not a high traffic day to go to the Peninsula. The tug I had felt earlier that morning was loosening its grip on my intestines as the boat inched its way closer to home and I felt the slightest feeling of relief as I sat in one of the many empty booths near the front of the main galley. The relief however was fleeting as a shiver ran down the back of my neck. As I glanced to my right I saw a family of three on the opposite side of the ferry's indoor cabin. A man in his early forties was talking quietly on his cell phone while a little girl I assumed was about four years old sat in the bench across from him playing with her doll. But standing completely still between them and staring directly at me was a woman in her early thirties with a warning look in her eyes. She was a slightly pale grey compared to the glow of life that emanated from the others. The man was completely oblivious to her presence but the little girl shyly looked over at me and then up at the woman and sadly went back to playing with her doll. And while I had no intention of intruding on this motherless family, the words "they are mine" rang clearly in my mind as the specter made sure that her warning not to encroach on her people was heard loud and clear. I politely turned away, avoiding her menacing stare, to look out the window instead at the black water rolling under the slow progress of the ferry.

These types of specters had been visible to me for as long back as I could remember, although the realization that I was the only one who could see them came when I was just three years old. My mother, Deidre, raised me on her own after my father died, in a small Victorian house uptown on Adams Street. She labored tirelessly restoring it in the evenings after she had worked all day in her antique store on the waterfront downtown. She catered to tourists during the day with their drippy ice cream cones and spicy pizza from the shop next door. Then, in the evening, after cooking dinner on our woodstove and putting me to bed, she would slowly refinish the old wood floors or restore the stained glass windows in the green carriage house. It was in this house that I had my first experience that I can clearly remember of interacting with a ghost. I sat at the edge of the parlor threshold still in the light of the living room and spoke with a man named Fox who could usually be found in the evenings sitting in the darkened room that was rarely used.

One night he told me where to find my Uncle Morgan's chess board, which had been collecting dust in a drawer, and how to set it up so he could teach me to play. After dutifully fetching the chess set, I began setting it up per Fox's instructions with me on the side of the doorframe with the light on and him on the other side in the dark. As I put the last few pieces perfectly in place, my Mother walked into the room and stared mouth open at the board. She carefully asked, "Charlotte, how did you know how to set up the chess board?" and with three-year-old honesty I simply replied, "Fox showed me" and pointed into the dark room.

Mayhem then ensued as my Grandfather George was called over to check and see if a man was hiding somewhere in the locked house, but alas there was just me and Deidre who realized that I, too, had found my Winship gift just like she and all the members of our family before us.

From that moment on I understood that the seemingly innocuous people that had been my playmates were something that grownups were afraid of and though most parents would have simply dismissed the incident as a fluke, my Mother knew better. From that moment on she acknowledged Fox by name and called him my guardian ghost. Fox became a permanent part of my day-to-day routine and while he seemed attached to the house, specifically the parlor, I felt that he was near me throughout most of my days and nights. His presence was calming and was sometimes accompanied by the faint smell of cloves and freshly cut wood. Although I never remember actually seeing him as an apparition, I could close my eyes and imagine his overall form as he wandered through the house or sat smoking a pipe in the Victorian chair in the parlor.

The boat began to shudder, jolting me from my daydreams of childhood as the engine slowed upon approach. The first light of day was just coming up over the mountains and there was a vibrant orange glow in the sky that was peeking through the perpetually grey October cloud cover. The outline of the Seattle skyline grew more distant as the boat headed on its path north. Soon all that could be seen was vast amounts of deep salt water with logs rolling in the boat's wake and fast approaching land that was populated by forests of evergreens.

As the ferry pulled into the dock and my car was liberated from the huge boat, like Jonah making a quick escape from the inside of a whale, I felt a rush of exhilaration that had been gone for years as I hit land again. Not just any land but my land. My home that I had been hiding from for three years for fear of what, I wasn't sure. Winding down the two-lane highway through the forest, as the light began to chase me through fast moving grey clouds, I tried to conjure an image in my mind of Morgan safe and unharmed but was met with only darkness. Grief had not yet sunk in, especially since Uncle Morgan's fate was still a mystery. But as I wove down the wet road with the smell of burning wood in the air all around, I had the strangest feeling that I was not alone in making this journey.

Normally a spirit making an appearance in the car is not as unusual as one might think. There is a stretch of highway near Deception Pass where a ghostly hitchhiker tags along accompanied by the peculiar smell of cigar smoke that fills the backseat. The presence I was feeling was far more powerful and I was overcome with an urgency to get home as quickly as possible. I was sure that something was following close behind in my wake, trying to catch up or prevent me from reaching my family -- although for what reason I had no inkling. And yet after hours of being awake my eyelids were getting heavy. Despite my sudden anxiety about the presence, a quick stop just up the road in Port Gamble for a cup of coffee was non-negotiable if I was going to make it to my Grandmother Margot's in one piece.

After a long stretch of straight highway the signs reducing the speed limit began to appear more rapidly. Then came the familiar bend in the road and a row of pristine Victorian homes that had been converted into an assortment of antique and artisanal shops appeared before me. Despite the growing sensation of being followed, it seemed that the tiny one street town was beckoning me to take a moments' rest before continuing along the road to home.

CHAPTER 3

It was still quite early in the morning when I arrived in Port Gamble. I had parked on the main street that made up the heart of the town. The entire charming avenue was lined with maple trees ablaze in this year's sudden autumn scarlet. They hovered protectively above the delicate Victorian homes that had been converted into quaint shops. The General Store was on the far end and served the purpose of café, local meeting spot, and unique boutique for the more discerning tourists. It also housed a shell museum that was organized in the original 19th century cabinets and dioramas. The sea life oddities were tucked away on the balcony of the second level. This was probably one of the few places in the world that could boast ownership of a stuffed gooey duck. But today, crab cadavers and giant nautiluses were the farthest thing from my mind. My search was for copious amounts of deliciously strong black coffee, so the disappointment was all the more palpable when I reached the door and a closed sign hung in the window. I shouldn't have been all that surprised since most shops on the Peninsula don't open until at least 10 a.m., but three years of Seattle life had spoiled me in its "coffee on every corner, day or night" mantra. I was still a few hours shy of the magical moment when the General Store would open. Despite that cruel fact, I cupped my hands to look through the old windows hoping someone would be kind enough to give me something caffeinated. Sadly all the lights were off inside.

Finally I resolved myself to getting back in the car with a plan to roll down all the windows and crank up the sounds of grunge in order to stay awake. That was when I noticed a flicker of light across the street. It was accompanied by the sudden appearance of a familiar face opening up the front door of the crooked yellow house on the corner. With her white hair tied up in an elaborate bun and her tiny body wrapped in a knit sweater, Beatrice Maddow almost flew out the door to my side with girlish squeals that filled the morning hush of the street.

Bee had been my Grandmother Margot's best friend since they were old enough to walk and talk which meant over 70 years and counting. She still ran her own shop in Port Gamble selling homemade honey, jams, lavender oil, and other local favorites. She had been raising bees her whole life so it was a quick step for all the locals to go from the name Beatrice to just plain Bee. And while the tourists loaded up their shopping baskets with all her sweets, the locals knew that what Bee was best at was figuring out the ways of love. If you had a broken heart, Bee would wrap a piece of rose quartz with red threads. Each suture was stitched with the intent to ease the pain and heal the wound. If you couldn't stop thinking about a certain someone she would create a special bath of rose petals, orange peels and other secret ingredients that once bathed in would attract your desired lover to you. And if you were searching for true love she would create a little figure out of her precious beeswax with a tiny ruby chip where the heart should be and a list of precise instructions to call your soul mate to you. This was how she had called her own soul mate Al to her from halfway around the world almost fifty years ago.

There wasn't a day that went by that Bee and Margot didn't talk for at least an hour on the phone. The conversations often stretched over several intervals and ranged in subject from what birds were nesting in Margot's attic to what new flavor of honey Bee was hoping to concoct. So when she ran up to me and gave me a welcome hug, I was sure that coffee was probably already boiling up in the percolator. She pulled me towards the open door of her shop with so much vigor it was hard to imagine that she was technically a little old lady.

"Coffee should be ready any second and you look like a cup wouldn't hurt," chirped Bee as we passed the threshold of her shop.

"You know I can't resist liquid gold at 8 a.m.," I sighed as we made our way inside. Bee's shop was lined with beautifully wrapped jars on white shelves. Her husband, Al, had built them all for her back when she first opened. She still heated the whole shop with a wood burning stove that was tucked in the back corner next to her rocking chair. Today there was another chair set out next to it and two cups waiting dutifully on a small tea caddy.

"Margot had an odd inkling that you were coming last night

when we spoke so I thought I would put an extra cup out for you. She didn't know why until the horrible news came in this morning," Bee said as she followed my glance towards the extra place setting before motioning for me to sit. "I can't tell you much more about Morgan's condition except to say that we will be there for the funeral on Friday. I will be praying for a miracle," she paused before handing me a small box. "Can you give this to Margot, dear?"

I imagined that the package contained one of her charms. Possibly for a broken heart. Bee had always said that a mother's broken heart is all but impossible to mend when a child is lost. I could only hope that Bee's charm would at least help to assuage some of Margot's pain in the immediate future if Morgan was truly gone. I all but collapsed into the chair feeling drained for the first time. My adrenalin from the 3am wake-up call was starting to wane and the gravity of the situation was beginning to sink in. Bee handed me my coffee black the way I liked it. I let myself feel the warmth of it in my hands while breathing in the earthy aroma in the hopes that it would keep me grounded.

"Bee, was it an accident with fire? I know nothing about what happened," I asked feeling a mix of anxiety and irritation at having been left in the dark.

"You really need to talk to Margot about these things dear," replied Bee in just the right way as to avoid giving any details. I was sure Margot had asked her not to tell me anything. She and my mother would want to give me the news in person if it was truly as dire as it seemed to be. It was their way. Pressing Bee wouldn't get me far but my deepening worry was getting the better of me. Instead, I decided to bring up the other reason for my increased anxiety.

"I can't quite put my finger on it Bee, but since I got off the ferry I've had this feeling that something is following me." I tried my best to describe the sensation in the hopes that she would be able to decipher what it might be. "It's almost chasing behind me and it isn't one of my usual ghosts. It feels far more powerful. And I get the distinct impression that," I paused for a moment as I tried to find the best way to describe the foreboding, "it is trying to prevent me from reaching Port Townsend." So there, I thought. I had managed to say it aloud. That the presence was something more than a mere emotion constructed from my own anxiety. The only thing that had ever come close was on the day that Morgan had almost been burned alive by a mysterious fire. An overwhelming feeling of darkness permeated the air around us as he had fled the town. Since then, the world had only been home to the usual haunts for me until this moment.

Bee held her cup tight in her wrinkled hands. Sitting back she began to creak in her wooden rocking chair. Her eyes were closed as she let the chair move her back and forth in a calming rhythm. Her lips moved subtly in a soft murmur. This was her way of seeking otherworldly guidance in regards to my mysterious presence. While each of us had our methods of channeling information, it was all very personal. Bee may have been talking to someone in her mind or receiving pictures of events or just sensing the words but whatever she was doing, it was a well-honed process and I trusted her. This was also a perfect example of why I had come alone. James would have been so completely out of his element in this world of intuition and signs that I wouldn't have known how to act with him here. I needed to be able to just function like I always had on the Peninsula. To Bee, intuition was more than just a nudging feeling that was brushed aside; it was listened to in earnest and practiced like an art. I sipped my coffee and let the warmth fill me as Bee continued to search beyond the veil.

In the silence, my mind began to wander into dangerous territory as I started to imagine what harm could have come to Morgan. Again I tried to focus on where he was and all I felt was a vast emptiness. And yet I couldn't help but think that if he had died he would have come to me to at least say goodbye. Was he stuck somewhere in-between or had an accident taken him so quickly that he did not yet realize he was dead? I would know soon enough. As Bee continued to rock in her chair, eyes pinched closed and wrinkled hands clutching the wooden handles, I finished the last dregs of my second cup of coffee. Without ceremony her chair came to a sudden halt. Bee finally lifted her head and replied:

"I'm sure Margot will tell you more but there is definitely something following you home although I cannot tell you specifically what it wants. I do know that it is powerful and it is cloaked in some type of cloud or fog. You need to get yourself across that new bridge and back to Margot and Deidre. I just have a feeling in my bones that whatever is coming is bringing a storm along with it." Just then as if on cue the lights flickered on and off a few times and a rumble could be heard in the distance.

"Up you go! You need to get moving -- not that I don't want to keep you here with me," she said, and with a spry leap Bee was out of her chair. She rapidly packed up a huge bag of jams, honey, and one of everything else in her shop for me to take along. With a whirlwind of sudden activity she buzzed from shelf to shelf and finally handed me the bag of goods that would have been the envy of many a tourist or town member alike.

I forced myself out of the chair and followed Bee to the door. I knew once I crossed the threshold the presence I had been feeling would become clear again and with it the urgency to get home. So I lingered for just a moment in the safety of the doorway and let Bee give me another of her all-encompassing hugs.

"We're looking forward to meeting that man of yours soon," she smiled. "He has been keeping you away from us for too long." I felt a flush move up to my cheeks thinking about James. Quickly, I pushed my emotions away as I needed to focus on getting back home and facing the looming darkness that was soon to follow behind me. I said my quick goodbyes on the way to the car as Bee watched me pull out and head in the direction of the bright green signs that exclaimed: Port Townsend 32 miles. I could see her in my rear view mirror looking up at the sky just as the first drops of rain began to fall.

Chapter 4

It was only a few miles to the Hood Canal Bridge but the rain had gone from a few drops to torrential in less than a minute. My windshield wipers were at maximum speed and this type of sudden storm coupled with wind was even unusual by Pacific Northwest standards. The forecast had been for the typical cloudy skies with scattered showers when I had left the house only a few hours earlier. The thought that supernatural elements were at work in keeping me from getting home only added to my growing anxiety.

I had to slow down as I made the turnoff onto the mile-and-a-half long bridge that linked the peninsula to the mainland. My heart caught in my throat when I noticed waves breaching the railings and splashing onto the empty roadway. There were no other cars to be seen on the long stretch of bridge that floated on the Puget Sound waterway. As I hit the gas and held my breath it was hard not to think of the fate of the old bridge three years earlier. I could still recall the images of the section of bridge that had been swept away to sea and the torn concrete and rebar that was left reaching out into the void to reclaim its lost limb.

Even though I was not in the habit of talking to myself out loud, I began to repeat the words "I will reach land safely, the wind and the waves can't touch me. The land awaits my return," in the hopes of calming my nerves while getting across the behemoth before the inevitable closing of the bridge. To avoid another disaster, if winds went above 50 miles per hour the bridge was automatically closed which would leave me stranded on the mainland. The wind across the straights was pushing the waves dangerously high onto the bridge and I could feel the rumble and sway of the new concrete shifting from side to side under my car. Stepping down on the accelerator and ignoring the slick metal grating that made my car swerve from side to side I kept my grip on the wheel as the other side of the bridge was nearing. Just as my car hit solid ground I noticed the sudden flashing red lights illuminated in my rear view mirror alerting the dropping of the no-passing guard rails. I had made it just in time. I quickly pulled my car off to the side of the road to catch my breath and stop my hands from shaking uncontrollably.

I had to admit that part of the shaking was probably due to the massive amounts of caffeine I had ingested since waking. The other part was the sense that I had escaped something's reaching grasp. I could picture a clawed hand reaching out to grab my car as I sped over those last few metal grates. It had been coupled with the same feeling of being followed from moments earlier. The second I hit land it retreated, cut off by my arrival on my element. I got out of the car and let the rain soak me threw as I squinted trying to see if there was anything on the other side of the bridge. It was completely empty other than the flashing red lights signaling that the bridge was closed until further notice. The lonely bridge controller was the only other soul I could spot as he stared nervously at the raging ocean from above in his metal tower.

I wondered to myself what Uncle Morgan must have felt as he had rushed in the opposite direction across the old bridge three years earlier with fire on his heels and the smell of burning hair all around him. There had always been something dark about Uncle Morgan, an indescribable presence that seems to hover on the periphery. My mother Deidre was like a little ball of yellow light where her twin brother Morgan was a strange mix of purplish-grey to my eyes. And unlike the usual grey ghosts that I spied from street corners to attic windows in detailed human likeness, the presence that was around Morgan had no real form but followed him everywhere like a cursed shadow. It was attached in an ethereal way and with it a feeling of dread and the smell of burning leaves and singed hair always clung to his pale skin.

From the time I was able to walk I treaded carefully around my Uncle Morgan. He was often pensive and lived on the outskirts of town in a tiny wooden farm house with a detached cider mill that had been built in the early 1900s. His cider was a local specialty as were his blackberry and dandelion wines as each had their own peculiar effect once imbibed. His apple cider was a perfect blend of sweet and sour with a hint of the smell of burning wood that would linger for hours on the taste buds and remove all inhibitions. His blackberry wine was thick and coated the mouth stimulating all the senses and often provoked a deep sense of longing either to pursue a long forgotten artistic passion or to rekindle a former love affair. But his dandelion wine was the most peculiar as he cultivated the flowers in the abandoned cemetery that bordered his land. It would inspire long evenings of conversation about the departed and often left the drinker feeling rooted again and at home wherever they were. But most people went to see him to read their future.

It was not something that anyone spoke of openly in town but everyone knew that Morgan was the one to see if you had lost your taste for life and needed a glimpse into the future. Usually people would sneak off down the winding road that had forest to one side and the Pacific Ocean on the opposite in the late hours of the night. Morgan was usually up from dusk till dawn. It was therefore normal to find him at the old apple press or kindling his woodstove while reading a book at three o'clock in the morning. He usually knew when someone would come rapping on his door twisted with guilt, grief or longing. And while he would look over his cards and listen to the whispers in the darkness around him there was always a cool detachment to Morgan as he looked on the lost souls that came to him for guidance. To the casual onlooker I am sure that Morgan seemed like nothing more than the town crazy but to me I saw a man haunted and also dangerously powerful in his abilities to manipulate not only people but the very fabric of his existence.

Now standing on the bridge soaked through with the pouring rain and ripping winds I couldn't help but wonder if he had unleashed something on us all. I quickly got back in the car, water dripping from the tips of my long hair and my body chilled to the bone. Soon I was back to speeding along the winding two way highway that was lined thick with evergreen forest and the occasional farm or church along the way. There were familiar landmarks like the Country Café, a greasy spoon that had been sitting at the same crossroads for as long as I could remember. There were also the more recent additions of drive-thru coffee huts. With the new bridge up, the tourists had been slowly coming back to the Peninsula which meant that the struggling towns were finally feeling the clenched fist of isolation releasing its grip on their livelihoods.

When I saw the drive-in movie billboard with its often missing letters and battered screen I knew I was almost home. The smell of the paper mill was also a less charming reminder of one of the town's main sources of employment along with the lumber mill and the wooden boat manufacturers. When I saw the "Entering Port Townsend" sign my body was filled with the strangest combination of relief and nausea. I was home again after three years of creating a wonderfully normal life in Seattle for myself with a charming man and a thriving business. Now I wondered what I was driving home into as I maneuvered the final stretch of highway into the strange little town with all its quirky residents and long buried secrets.

Chapter 5

On the bluff entering into town there are two things that one immediately sees, on the right is a spectacular view of the bay with the steep winding road that leads to the downtown area of Port Townsend. And on the left a massive edifice that overlooks it all called Eisenbeis Monastery.

Eisenbeis Castle was built in 1892 by the family of the same name who wanted to bring the feel of their native home in the Black Forests of Germany to this far off part of the new world. They were the closest thing to a feudal lord that the 19th century could provide as they owned much of the town and were the main reason that Port Townsend had been built with a certain grandeur that the other logging towns lacked. But the grandest of all the homes and buildings was undoubtedly their own Eisenbeis Castle with its 30 rooms, private chapel and expansive view of the town. It was a tribute not only to their wealth but also to the high hopes that the Eisenbeis family had for the tiny town they called their new home. Sadly these dreams never came to fruition when the patriarch, Charles, died suddenly of a strange fever after completing the last of the construction on the castle. His wife Kate was left alone wandering the endless empty rooms until her death shortly after. The castle itself sat empty until in 1927 a group of Jesuit priests purchased the rundown castle to use as a monastery.

I avoided the Eisenbeis Monastery for a number of reasons, firstly my Grandmother Margot had a mysterious falling out with the Catholic Church around the time Deidre and Morgan were born and it had been passed down as a family tradition. This was not to say that Margot was not a true Catholic in her heart and still deeply devoted to the Madonna but something had been broken irrevocably and she refused to speak of it with the exception of forbidding any Winship from visiting the monastery and its monks. And while I normally would have been tempted to rebel against this type of authority, I had always been aware of a certain presence around the castle that I did not want to be in close proximity to. Every time I would pass by there would always be a solitary figure of a monk in black robes standing on the edge of the castle grounds staring blankly and seemingly unable to cross the threshold that marked the property of the monastery.

Today was no different and as I glanced to the left through the pouring rain I could see the same melancholic specter standing at the edge of the property with his hand reaching out to me, begging for my attention. Usually if the dead had a message for me they tended to make themselves known in numerous ways and for as long as I can remember this monk spirit had been trying desperately to get my attention every time I passed by. Deep down I knew that Margot had a good reason for wanting the Winships to stay far away from this place so I did as always and turned my gaze back to the winding road that led to the heart of the town. I could always feel his stare burrowing into me until I had safely rounded the corner and was out of view of the castle. Today was no different and I felt a certain amount of relief after passing out of sight of the monk ghost although the sense of being followed was still lingering.

I stepped on the gas and sped through the downtown area knowing that I would be through later in the day to say hello to old friends and curious townsfolk. But for now my only thought was to get to Margot's and find out what had happened to Morgan. The town was still cloaked in rain torn sleep and the familiar sounds of waves crashing on the shore along with the faint ringing of the old bell tower in the wind. In a few hours the downtown area, which was spread out along one long street that was bordered with beach front on one side and cliffs on the other, would be bustling with the promise of a newly rejuvenated commerce. Even in my rush to get through the main road and up the hill to Willow Street I couldn't help but notice at least ten new shops lined up beautifully in the rows of Victorian buildings which included Deidre's own long standing antique shop perched on the corner of Main Street. Quickly I left the shops behind me and wound my way towards my Grandmother's home. Uptown was set on top of the cliffs on Willow Street where the Winship House had its spot among the other majestic Victorian ladies.

Up ahead I could see the pink turret skirted with woodwork

that resembled white lace from a distance. The massive iron fence that lined the Winship property had taken on a reddish hue due to the many years of rain and saltwater air that thrashed the cliffs. Swaying in the wind was the hundred year old weeping willow that had been cherished among all the Winship women. It had grown nearly as tall as the weather vane on the third story of the imposing pink house. As I pulled into the long gravel driveway and made my way to park near the carriage house I could feel a sense of protection and ease come over me. This house was under the watchful eye of Margot Winship and of all the places in the world this was the one spot on earth where I felt safest.

I made a quick dash for the front door, leaving my bag behind for later, and skipped the one loose step on my way up to the covered porch. Just as I flipped my hood off and looked to open the screen door, I was surprised to find Margot waiting with the door already open. I couldn't help but fold myself into her arms like a child just to breathe in the wonderful smell of roses that hovered around her as she quickly ushered me into the house.

Before I could even get my coat hung on the rack by the door I blurted out, "What happened?" My nerves were beginning to fray between the 3am wake-up call and the feeling of being chased across the bridge. I had just about had enough with all the secrecy.

"First come in and sit," was Margot's stern response and I felt immediately foolish for thinking I could rush right into things. Margot had a certain formality to her so I followed her through the long front hallway that was filled almost floor to ceiling with images of our ancestors both photographic and painted. All the eyes were watching us as we made our way to the one room in the house where serious discussions were inevitably held, the kitchen. I took my familiar seat which was the chair at the huge oak round table closest to the wood stove. I could hear the familiar crackling of a log that was more than half burnt down.

Margot eased herself into her chair and for the first time since arriving I looked straight into her troubled green eyes. The thin lines that had formed since I had left three years ago were joined by red rings indicating a sleepless night. For the first time I could start to see her age reflected by a sense of weariness beneath the usually stern demeanor. With a deep sigh, she began to tell of what had happened to Morgan only a few hours earlier.

"This morning your Mother got a call from Jefferson Hospital that a man's body was found outside in the unloading zone of the emergency room." She said while looking down at her folded hands. "At first everyone thought he was dead because the body was so badly burnt that he was barely recognizable and had no identification on him. It was your Uncle Morgan and the only reason they called your mother is because Samir was on call and recognized the portion of his face that was the least burnt as well as the star birthmark on his shoulder that was completely untouched. He is in a coma and the doctors did not think that he would make it through the night and told us to begin funeral preparations. But he has been hanging on and Deidre is with him now. I just came home from the hospital knowing you would be arriving soon."

I felt the table tip slightly and the room started to shift as the news of what had happened to Morgan began to sink in to my sleep deprived senses. I could picture the unloading zone of the hospital emergency room all too well but the thought of his body on the ground under a pouring rain was almost too much to bear. I could see Margot struggling with the same emotions and the fact that he was still alive and trapped in a shell left me feeling nauseous as the smell of burnt leaves flashed through the room.

"Did anyone see anything?" I asked as it was hard to imagine someone driving up and dumping his body at the hospital without someone noticing, especially a hospital as small as the Port Townsend one.

"It was as if he simply appeared out of thin air," replied Margot. "One second they were rolling someone into emergency and the next there he was on the ground with what was left of his clothes still steaming. They were rolling him to the morgue when he made a sound."

We both sat in silence for a moment, mourning the devastating news. My eyes scanned the room to rest on a statue of the Madonna. Margot loved this effigy above all which was evident by its placement on a small table in the corner surrounded by at least twenty lit votive candles and several small bouquets of her garden roses on all sides. I imagined her kneeling before the Blessed Mother with her rosary beads moving in a steady rhythm through her arthritic hands as she prayed for her only son's life. For as long as I could remember Morgan had been trying to out run his element of fire. Now that it seemed like it had finally caught him I couldn't help but wonder what events had led to his unfortunate fate.

A shrill ring from the old rotary phone broke the silence. Margot answered with her usual "Winship Residence, this is Margot speaking." She listened quietly as I could vaguely make out my Mother's voice on the other line as Margot gently nodded her head along to the words being spoken. Her only answer was "Yes, she is safe," and finally "we will come by later" and then a quick "goodbye."

"They have moved him into a special sterile room and are trying to stabilize him through hydration," Margot announced as she hung up the phone. "You should get a bit of rest before we go over to the hospital, they won't let us in to see him now anyway," she said with a fatigue in her voice that gave me pause and additional worry. And then Margot added with a little smile and a quick glance to the Madonna statue "the doctors are saying it's a miracle he is alive...for now."

I could feel my eyelids getting suddenly heavy and the idea of curling up in a little ball in this home that felt so safe was an extremely tempting notion. If it hadn't been for the nagging sensation of something evil following on my heels I would have been halfway to my old room by now. As it was I thought that telling Margot about it took precedence over sleep.

"Margot, something odd happened on my way over. As soon as I got off the ferry and started towards Port Gamble I could feel something following me along with the storm. I almost didn't make it across the bridge and it wasn't just the circumstances of the trip home. I just have the nagging feeling that something is coming here and it means us harm." Just saying the words out loud gave me a sudden sense of relief but I could tell by Margot's face that the revelation of an unknown entity following me had her none too pleased.

"I sent the storm, Charlotte," replied Margot with a slight twitch of her left eye. "There is something coming for your Uncle Morgan. I wanted to slow it down with the storm but inevitably it will find a way to come. That is why you should get some rest."

Storms had been Margot's gift from the time she was just a small child much like my vision of spirits and my mother Deidre's messages from birds. Margot could conjure a nasty storm of wind, rain and ocean waves that could bring every vessel and whale alike to shore. There were stories of unusual storms on the coast after her birth and through her early years before she was able to learn how to control her emotions and focus her gift for more benevolent purposes. In the early years of her marriage to her husband George, my Grandfather, the town would joke whenever a spontaneous storm would appear by saying that Margot and George must be having a glitch in their seemingly perpetual honeymoon phase. But to think that she had sent this storm to keep something away from town was disconcerting and I couldn't help but feel that she was keeping something from me.

"Go get some rest dear," she said before I could ask more about the coming presence, "we will talk more later and for now I am just relieved that you are here safe, your Mother is with Morgan and I need to call Bee and tell her there will be no funeral on Friday as far as we know." Margot said the last part with a quiver in her voice that told me she wasn't as certain of her words as she would have liked me to believe.

"Upstairs you go," Margot said as she rose from her chair and I felt once again somewhat in the dark but my fatigue was beating out my stubbornness to know more. As I made my way up the long curving stairwell I couldn't help but say a little prayer under my breath for Morgan that his guardian angels had his soul to keep.

CHAPTER 6

The turret room of the Winship house had been my room for as long as I could remember. And even though I spent the majority of my nights sleeping in my Mother's house only two blocks away with Fox keeping a silent vigil, this room was always my other refuge.

When I moved to Seattle, my mother Deidre turned my old room into her art studio. She spent countless nights paying homage to the birds that came to her with messages by tucking them in-between tiny depictions of all the houses with their Victorian flare. So the turret room at the Winship house was now the one place that I could call my little corner. Most of my boxes of childhood memories were still residing in the dusty old Winship house attic amid boxes of my Great-Grandmother Elsiba's vintage clothes, random photo albums and trinkets dating back to the first days of the town's construction.

It was three flights up to the north facing turret. As I walked up each landing it struck me how absolutely nothing had changed in the three years since I had been gone. The wallpaper was still a deep burgundy with little Victorian stripes. The brass wall sconces were neatly polished and evenly spaced in the hallway and stairwell lighting every step in the 150 year old house. The first floor entrance of the Winship house was bordered by formal parlors to the left and right. They had also scarcely changed since the house was furnished by the first Winship woman. To the back of the house was the kitchen, a mudroom that led to the gardens, a formal dining room and an old fashioned water closet.

The second floor was a long hallway of bedrooms which included Margot's room that overlooked her rose garden in the back of the house. Morgan and Deidre's old bedrooms sat across from one another. My Grandfather George's library was at the opposite side of the house with its view of the downtown area below the cliff's edge and the water beyond. The third floor led to my turret room. There was also a small bathroom complete with a claw-foot tub on one side of the landing and a third door which led to the vast attic space that held generations of memories. I pushed open the old door to my room and was instantly greeted by the smell of roses. On the bedside table and the dresser were two large mixed color bouquets of Margot's roses, the fragrance of which were coveted throughout the town.

The pink roses had a sweetness that was intoxicating to some and many in town claimed that it could make a man drunk with love upon smelling a single bud. This may have been because the story of my grandparents' courtship began in the Winship rose garden one hot June day when the pink roses were in full bloom. Margot had been only seventeen when the strapping twenty year old George had been hired to trim the Winship willow tree. He had climbed high into the tangled branches and was trying to tame the massive tree when he spied Margot in her white summer dress picking a bouquet of pink roses below. He had been frozen with fear and longing all combined into one distracted emotion and as he shifted his weight to the side his foot slipped and he landed flat on his back only a few feet from where Margot stood. Naturally she was shocked to find such a handsome young man had actually fallen from the sky to her feet and she knelt to make sure that he wasn't badly hurt. The pink roses in the garden seemed to shake with excitement and the perfume that emanated from them wafted out into a three block radius leaving the neighbors overwhelmed with the lovesick feelings one can only have in their youth. From that day on they were by each other's side and the pink roses accompanied every anniversary party they celebrated for the forty one years they were married up until George's passing. It had become a kind of tradition for young lovers in town to try to steal a pink rose from Margot's garden to give to their beloved. Some attempts were more successful than others.

The red roses in Margot's garden were spicy and smelled of cardamom. They had rich velvety petals that verged on black. There was seductiveness to these buds that intrigued more than the other blooms. Their perfume often made people feel a deep desire for travel to far off places. Their thorns were the sharpest of the roses in the garden and Margot always came inside with pin pricks up her arms when she pruned them. She jokingly called them her little vampires.

And while the red rose was by far the most exotic of her garden in their teacup sized blossoms and rich aroma they were also to be handled with a certain care.

The yellow roses smelled fresh like summer rain. These had always been Margot's favorites as she bundled them into huge bouquets and left them on her friend's front porches when the rose bushes were full to breaking in August. The yellow roses left all who reveled in their cool perfume with an overall feeling of wellbeing and friendship. Often locals would ask Margot for a yellow rose to give to a friend after a feud. There were even longstanding family and neighborly disputes that were said to have been resolved with a bouquet of Margot's yellow roses.

There were these and all the colors in-between including climbing roses that stretched their vines along the sides of the house up to Margot's bedroom window, tea roses that hugged the stone walkways and even a strange night blooming rose that few knew existed in Margot's prized garden. And all these roses had another peculiarity in that they bloomed from May to December when the garden would promptly drop all its blossoms on the last day of advent. All the other flowers in Margot's garden followed the normal ebb and flow of the seasons. But the roses were stubborn and kept their perfumes and blossoms even when the snow was falling and the winds had thrashed all the trees of their leaves.

It was these roses that filled my room with their combined perfumes and lulled me to sleep under the covers of the four poster bed. I didn't even bother to take off my clothes. I climbed under the feather comforter still wearing jeans and a slightly damp shirt where I immediately fell into a deep sleep filled with vivid and disturbing dreams of the lone monk spirit. It was one of those dreams where everything was exactly as it is in reality. I was asleep in my bed and the monk spirit was standing at the bedside peering down at me with the same intensity as when I had seen him earlier that morning. He leaned down and whispered in my ear that he wanted me to wake up and follow him to the attic. "It's in the attic, Charlotte," he whispered, and suddenly we were at the attic door. I opened the door to the room piled high with not only all of my childhood memories stacked in a neat pile in the corner but the boxes belonging to everyone who had lived in this house before me. The monk made his way to a large box that was tucked behind an old wooden pram and pointed to it silently. In a flash the monk's face contorted into a grimace of pain that dropped him to his knees in front of me. He held his face in his hand and began to sob. As I put my hand on his shoulder I could smell the familiar odor of burning hair and leaves. When he looked up at me he was no longer the monk but rather Uncle Morgan with half his face burnt black.

I sat straight up in bed awake with my heart pounding and the strange sensation of expecting to be standing in the attic. It took a moment for me to place myself in time and space. Across the room, I looked out the window to see that the wind and rain had stopped and in its place a thick white fog had rolled into town. I made my way to the window and was surprised to see that I could hardly discern the familiar willow tree branches, as the fog was so dense. Its branches stretched up to surpass the turret and yet they were almost completely obscured. In the upper corner of the window a large spider web was glistening white as the fog had brought an icy chill along with it. My breath left a circle of steam on the window as I leaned in closer to try to see into the yard. That was when I noticed another breath mark on the window next to me only at my shoulder level and off to my left side. There was a presence in the room with me. As I stood stalk still I heard a child's voice whisper "The Strangers are coming."

CHAPTER 7

I was unsurprisingly unable to go back to sleep after the disturbing dream coupled with the message from the little girl ghost. I decided that a quick look in the attic would be the only thing that would quiet the unease that I felt. The way that the word "strangers" had sounded on her ghostly breath and the sudden icy fog that had come into town in the wake of Margot's storm gave me an even more foreboding sensation than before I had laid down to rest. In a small town there are three main groups by which people are labeled and the first is "local," the second is "tourist" and the third is "stranger." The latter was ripe with a fear and loathing that locals felt when someone, or in this case something, came to town with uncertain motives. But this appellation felt considerably more complicated in its meaning in the sense that it felt like the ghost was telling me the coming presence's name.

Any witch worth her salt, that is if a witch was what us Winships could be called, knows that a name holds tremendous power. It was one of the reasons that Winship women refused to give up their name upon marrying and also the reason that when a ghost or spirit would tell me it's, or another's name, I would always take great care to keep it as sacred. A name could be used in many positive ways but it can also be used to invoke, control and manipulate in a manner that few consciously understand yet many can feel on a deeper level. Such is the source of the old expression of having "burning ears" when others are talking about you. So the name "the Strangers" definitely caught my attention as did the dream about the monk and the box in the attic.

I quickly made my way into the hall and over to the attic door. As I reached out and turned the old porcelain knob I found the door locked for the first time that I could remember in all my years of wandering through this house. I wondered if Margot had taken to locking the doors now that she lived alone in such a large home. It left me with an unnerving sensation not to be able to at least ease my mind about the mysterious box in my dream.

Quietly I made my way downstairs in stocking feet and was shocked to see the time on the old grandfather clock in the second floor hallway. Its old hands pointed to just past 3 p.m. which meant I had been asleep for most of the morning and afternoon although it had felt like no more than ten or fifteen minutes since I had rested my head on my pillow. I could hear Margot's muffled voice downstairs most likely speaking with Bee on the phone. The words "coma" and "burnt" seemed to hang in the air like a curse.

When I rounded the last flight of stairs and made my way to the kitchen, Margot quickly told Bee to hang on a second and covered the phone with her hand to give me a quick update, "Charlotte, I just got off the phone with your Mother and they said that no one will be allowed near your uncle until a specialist is flown in from Seattle. She is going home to sleep a little but will be coming here tonight at 8 to give us more details."

"I might go into town for a bit but I'll be back before dark. Do you know where the key to the attic is?" I asked, not wanting to bother Margot with the details of why I wanted to go rummaging around after a box that appeared in my dream. I couldn't help but to be taken aback by the way that she suddenly sat up perfectly straight like something had pinched her when I mentioned the attic. She was staring at me in the most peculiar way and then quickly answered "it has been missing for three years, since your Uncle Morgan left." And then she simply went back to talking with Bee and ignored me completely.

Not wanting to disturb her further given her rather prickly mood, I found my shoes and purse and gave a quick wave before heading out the door to which she nodded. I just couldn't shake the feeling that she was keeping something from me as I made my way through the mist to my car. It would have to wait until later. After being away for three years I owed two people a visit as they were the next closest thing to my family, especially considering the events that had led to my return.

When I moved to Seattle three years ago my two best friends from childhood both loved-and-hated me for going but soon Gavin and

Kat got over it when they opened the "Waterside Brewery" together. It had been a completely unexpected turn of events for both of them when Gavin's Great Aunt passed away and left him an inheritance that was just enough to buy the huge old town tavern building which had been boarded up for more than ten years. In it they decided to start a small micro-brewery in half of the building while the front was turned into an ale house. Even in a bad economy the venture had done quite well as it was the one place in town where there was live music every weekend and enough of Gavin's wicked brew to keep all the loggers and fishermen satisfied when they came into town after a hard day's work. And now that the tourists were coming back Gavin could hardly keep up with production while Kat thrived on keeping the ale house bustling with new bands and strange local concoctions on their lunch and dinner menus.

We had been an unlikely trio growing up, most people simply didn't know how to act around me as I was often distracted by things others couldn't see or feel. But for some reason Gavin, Kat and I just fit together as friends in the most perfectly odd combination of personalities. Gavin was brilliant and his scientific curiosities always kept him scribbling in notebooks and looking into microscopes or later in high school mixing up moonshine for the school football team in order to pay for the piece of equipment that was his latest obsession. He was well over six feet tall, rail thin and had a pale complexion with a scruffy matt of un-kept blond hair that was always falling in his eyes or getting scorched by his Bunsen burner. And while he was considered rather ungainly when we were growing up when he and Kat had come to visit me in Seattle only a few months earlier I couldn't help but notice he had grown into himself and had become quite handsome in a quiet way.

Kat on the other hand was a social butterfly with an edge; she came from another of the founding families, although unlike the Winships, the Starrets were one of the more respected families in town. She was expected to play her part in keeping with certain family traditions like being a "Rhododendron Queen" which consisted of riding on a float through town every spring and doing a number of other displays of popularity. Instead she shocked everyone in town by insisting on spending her time with Gavin and myself or locked in her bedroom writing melancholic music. When she took on the role of running the ale house portion of her and Gavin's business her family was furious that she would even think of spending her life working in a bar. She was expected to marry one of the town doctors or at least go off to the university for four years but being that Kat was one of the most stubborn people the town had ever known, with exception to Margot, they soon realized it was a losing battle and grudgingly gave in to her decision. With her bright red hair dyed pink on one side and her humor tinged with just the right amount of sarcasm, she had always been the one person I knew who would be entirely honest with me while remaining fiercely loyal.

I, just by the name Winship alone, had been treated with certain wariness by the rest of the town since the discovery of my gift. This is not to say that I wasn't one of them in a very profound way because I fell into the category of both "local" as well as being from one of the founding families of Port Townsend. But people just knew that I could see things that others couldn't and that I received messages from the departed that I often had to pass along to family members. This was always an awkward situation when I would be awoken in the middle of the night by a recently deceased townsperson who needed me to tell this or that to the remaining wife, husband or child. The messages could be anything and ranged from the somewhat humorous, like Mr. Comos insisting I tell his wife that he had hidden $13,000 in cash in a false wall in their bathroom, to the more delicate message of Mrs. Elroy to her former lover that the son she had claimed to have by Mr. Elroy really belonged to him. So naturally when I came walking up people's driveways at odd hours not long after someone in town had passed away they all expected a secret to be revealed. What they didn't know was that I had no choice but to pass these messages on because the dead are horribly insistent and simply won't leave until I fulfill their request. So by some miracle I had Gavin and Kat when I just needed to be a normal kid and later teenager as they were the two people outside of family that knew me as more than just the girl that heard the secrets that people took to their graves.

It was with my two best friends in mind that I juggled my car keys from my purse. Hopefully Kat and Gavin would be able to give me some piece of mind or at least lend me a loving ear. My stomach was a knot of nerves as I imagined Uncle Morgan hooked up to machines on the other side of town. It was bad enough to not know what his fate would be but the addition of the ghost messages was only adding to my anxiety. I also needed to call James and let him know that I had arrived in Port Townsend but my nerves were keeping me from talking to him. He would hear the stress in my voice and want to know the details of what was wrong and I just couldn't open that can of worms just yet. Thankfully Kat and Gavin were only a five minute drive from the Winship house. I felt a flutter of excitement at seeing them as I climbed back into my car and pulled out of the fog-obscured driveway.

CHAPTER 8

With my headlights on high beams to cut through the thick white fog I wound my way down the hill. Taking a left at the bell tower the two lane road curved towards downtown with a serpentine twist. I could hear the fog horns booming on the waterfront to warn vessels of the nearness of land. The town had woken up since I had driven through earlier as was evidenced by the hustle and bustle of cars and people filling the small downtown streets. I parked north of the front door of the ale house and was shocked to see how beautifully Gavin and Kat had restored the old brick building. Even through the ever thickening fog, I could see the glowing stained glass windows above the corner door and the original "town tavern" mural still on one side of the brick building. Just as I opened the door I heard Kat let out a shriek from behind the fifteen foot oak bar. She ran over to me and gave me a squeeze that left me breathless, for such a tiny little person she could pack a serious hug.

"Lottie, what are you doing here?" she asked, genuinely surprised to see me. She was the only person in the world that was allowed to give me a nickname. It was a habit of hers that had become endearing over time although she once tried to call Margot "Grams" but she had received a look that made even Kat bite her tongue.

"I thought word traveled fast in these parts," I said. She looked at me with a surprised stare.

"Lottie, why don't you go sit at the corner table and I'll finish up with a few orders then we can talk," she motioned to an empty round wooden table set a little father off to the side of the bar near the side street windows. Even in the afternoon there were only a few empty spots at the bar and the tables were half filled as well, mostly with loggers and a few tourists. As I settled into the corner table a few of the people I knew from town gave me little nods and even a wink or two. Kat filled a series of pitchers of Gavin's brew and then ran into the back room. She came back out with a basket and two glasses of a dark red liquid that I could only imagine was one of their latest inventions.

"I know these are your favorites," she said as she set the checkered wax paper lined basket filled with breaded and fried local razor clams on the table. They were my favorite and just the smell of the grease made my head spin. There were certain tastes and smells that are irrevocably linked to home.

"So what ARE you doing all the way back here? Not that I am not happy to see you," Kat added with a smile. "Are things ok with James?" she added as she settled into the wooden backed chair. Her question reminded me again that I hadn't called James since I had gotten into town. I was sure that he was probably frantic with worry by now which made me feel a wave of guilt.

I proceeded to tell her everything that had transpired since three a.m. that morning in-between much needed bites of clams and sips of the most incredible beer I had ever imbibed. I was not a drinker but this was definitely taking the edge off of the stress and anxiety that had been fueling my energy up until this moment. When I finished I noticed that she wasn't the only one listening in on the story. The bar had a constant rumble of noise of deep men's voices booming up through the 20 foot ceilings and the occasional woman's laugh. But in the corners and up in the archways of the second floor balcony there were three figures, one man and two women, who stood unmoving while fixing me with ghostly stares. The man was standing in the center of the stage towards the back of the bar. It was where the band played on the weekends although today it was empty but for this single male figure who was slightly greyer than the lively people that were drinking all around completely oblivious to his presence. I could feel his eyes fix on me while his face was expressionless.

There was also a woman in the far corner of the bar that was staring at me with what could almost be a look of fright. She was dressed in a flimsy slip and had an obvious wound in her neck. Her hand instinctively pressed against the gash to stop what I presumed was the hemorrhage that had taken her life. And the final figure was also a woman looking down from the balconies which was now the second floor pool room. I was pretty sure the upper rooms had been part of the turn of the century bordello that was once in the town tavern. She also had a sharp eye on me and a stern face.

"Holy shit Lottie," Kat said while letting out a sigh. "I'm so sorry to hear about Morgan. I've kind of been in my little bubble all day and I hadn't heard a thing."

"I should know more tonight but I have to admit that I am sort of reeling from everything. I can't even believe I am back here and I haven't called James," I said, feeling my cheeks redden. "Also I had the weirdest dream and then a message about something or someone called 'the Strangers', coming to town?" I added.

A sudden hush came over the bar. It wasn't as if everyone had stopped talking but rather like the volume of everyone's voices and movements in the room had suddenly been turned down. Then I heard the three ghosts begin to whisper in slow intervals "the Strangers, the Strangers, the Strangers" increasing rapidly in frequency. The man on the stage walked backwards until he faded into the wall and the woman in the corner turned and ran from the room as if chased by an unseen attacker. The last woman in the balcony kept repeating "the Strangers" until she suddenly stopped and put her index finger up to her mouth and made a "shhh" noise to mean silence before she also retreated into the shadows of the balcony arches and the chanting stopped. The volume of the room returned to normal but the chill that I felt over my whole body was very real. I noticed that the light was starting to fade outside and the fog was thicker than ever.

"Kat, I have to get back to the house," I said, realizing I had been there for almost two hours telling her the details of the day and that I wanted to get back before dark. "Can you tell Gavin what is going on and I will call or come by tomorrow?" I said, feeling extremely uneasy about the fading light outside and the ghosts' reaction to my speaking the name "the Strangers."

"Of course, I will stop by the house later tomorrow or we'll see you here," she said as I quickly gave her a hug, threw on my jacket and made my way to the front door. I hadn't noticed but the bar was almost completely full and several of the servers where lighting the little votive candles on each table as the dimming light outside was signaling a shift in mood.

Stepping out onto the street, I noticed the immediate silence after the door to the noisy bar shut behind me. The shops were all closing and turning off their lights as they packed away their wares for the coming night. As I quickly made my way to the car I noticed on both sides of the street and in the upstairs windows of the Victorian facades pale grey faces peering down at me. The same whisper repeating on their lips like a fearful mantra "the Strangers, the Strangers, the Strangers." It mixed into the mist and left me with a feeling of dread as I fumbled my keys twice before opening the car door and hurriedly made my way back to the Winship house. The voices echoed in my ears like a hum on the creeping fog. All the town ghosts were whispering together as I raced up the hill and pulled into the long driveway. I ran to the front door even though the fog was so thick that I could hardly see a few feet in front of me. Once inside I immediately locked the door behind me and leaned breathless against the hallway wall.

I felt a wave of gratitude that the house was silent with the exception of a crackle of fire in the kitchen stove. I imagined that Margot was resting before Deidre came over with more news on Morgan's condition. I tiptoed up the steps making sure not to wake anyone as the voices of the town ghosts were still lingering in my mind. Just as I made my way to the landing of the third floor and was heading to my room I heard the distinct click of a lock as I passed by the attic door. I stopped immediately in my tracks. I glanced warily over to the door that had been locked tight earlier in the evening. My heart thumped rapidly in my chest as it slowly creaked open a few inches beckoning me to venture inside.

CHAPTER 9

For a moment I simply stood staring at the once locked door that had ever so sneakily opened of its own accord. Having become accustomed since childhood to seeing strange things I shouldn't have been as frozen with fear as I was in this moment. Although with the words "the Strangers" still hovering in the air and the dream of the monk still fresh in my mind the now wide open door left me feeling on edge. Carefully I inched my way closer to the door expecting someone to jump out from behind it. As I lightly pushed it open and flipped on the light I could clearly see that no one dead or alive was hiding amid the piles of forgotten Winship memories.

As I scanned the room while standing perfectly still my eyes fell to the exact spot that the monk had shown me in the dream. A wooden pram covered with dust sat primly in the corner and tucked just behind it was the large box. I carefully made my way to it still feeling on edge and before getting too far inside the attic door I shoved a large book in the doorjamb to keep the door from shutting and locking me in. The box itself was unremarkable on the outside and had no writing or features that made it anything more than just a plain cardboard box that smelled of mildew. I carefully removed the tape that sealed the top and inside the first thing that I saw were two sets of tiny shoes. Inside of each pair was written "Morgan" and the other "Deidre" in Margot's beautiful script. They sat perched on top of my mother's and Morgan's baby clothes all folded neatly into delicate squares of soft cotton. As I slowly removed them I found an album dated 1953 with a beautifully embossed cover and silk tassels binding the pages together.

The first page held one of my favorite pictures of my grandparents Margot and George with cheeks pressed together looking straight into the camera. It was one that my mother had used to make an original painting for their 40th wedding anniversary as there were already several copies of this picture framed around the house. As I thumbed through the black pages I couldn't help but remember some of the moments I had spent with my Grandfather George before he had passed.

George mowed the lawn and kept up the cemetery for free during his retirement years. I would often go with him while he worked, running from grave to grave in what most children considered the scariest part of town. It was an unusual place for a small child to want to play but with George working nearby it felt peaceful. This probably hadn't helped with the "Graves" nickname and the fear that I seemed to inspire in many of the town's children, with the exception of Kat and Gavin.

This is probably why the graveyard held so much comfort for me as a place to just be and while one would think that graveyards would be rife with wandering ghosts I always found it to be quite the opposite. What was buried beneath did not usually linger above. Instead the only thing that seemed to hover was energy that made the air a bit thicker with emotion. I was particularly drawn to the children's graves which included a special section with a tiny white picket fence that enclosing them in an eternal crib. My Grandfather and I weeded by hand to avoid damaging the delicate wood spindles with the lawn mower. In this area I was always visited by a tiny striped kitten that would pounce out of the nearby bushes and sit with me while I worked. No matter the number of years that went by the kitten was always the same and would brush against me and play with me and quietly peer up at me with knowing eyes until it was time for me to go home. While skipping through the graveyard the kitten would follow and I could hear in the wind the sounds of people laughing and playing with me while my grandfather cleaned the graves and made sure that all the dead flowers were removed and the new flowers had water.

Now looking at these black and white images of my grandparents in their youth I couldn't help but feel a chill pass through me at the thought of George being a part of that cemetery now. As I thumbed through the progression of images it became clear that Margot was becoming increasingly pregnant as the photos went along. And then as I neared the last page, I felt a surge of adrenaline flood through my body as I happened upon a photo of Margot standing in the gardens of the Eisenbeis Monastery next to an elderly priest. They had a magnificent rose bush between them and both were smiling and gesturing towards the plant. But what gave me a chill was that in the background of the photo the monk from my dream, except very much alive, was standing on the periphery staring at Margot with an intensity that made the hair on my neck stand on end.

Had they known each other? Was it possible that he was one of the reasons that Margot had forbidden Winships from visiting the Eisenbeis Monastery? These and a million other questions raced through my mind. As I reached down into the now almost empty box there sat a large black paper folder nearly four inches thick. It was bound with a cord and a wax seal from the Eisenbeis Monastery that had never been broken. A tiny paper was folded into fours and slid under the cord and as I opened it the words read:

> *My dearest Margot,*
> *Forgiveness will set you free.*
> *Sincerely,*
> *Father Benedict*

All I could think was that whoever this Father Benedict was he must not have known my Grandmother Margot very well because she definitely knew how to hold a grudge. I quickly turned back to the last page of the photo album and carefully removed the black and white picture from its photo corners. Examining the back revealed words written in Margot's curled and looped handwriting that read "*Me and Father Benedict August 15th, 1953.*"

I looked back at the sealed file that Margot had never opened but rather had packed up into a box of baby clothes and left in the attic to gather dust. I couldn't help but wonder why if she hadn't wanted it had she kept it all these years but never opened it? My fingers started to tremble as I lifted it and set it on my lap. I knew that I would have to open it or the monk spirit would come back until I did, this was how these things worked, but why now? I had been seeing the monk spirit since I was a child on the grounds of the Eisenbeis Monastery and while he had tried to get my attention before he had never stepped into my dreams until today.

Quickly I pulled up on the cord and broke the seal before I lost my nerve. I paused, expecting Margot to come crashing into the attic livid that I had trespassed on something that she hadn't dared to open. Instead silence filled the house. The first page that I pulled out was cut from the Port Townsend Reader which is the one and only town newspaper. It was dated Nov. 8th, 1953 and it read:

Fruitless Search for Priest's Body
On this most tragic of days Nov. 4th, the visiting priest Father John O'Malley, SJ is believed drowned after attempting to swim the unforgiving local waters. For the past six months he has been a guest of the Eisenbeis Monastery while attended special classes. After announcing to his fellow priests that he would be venturing out for a swim on the evening of Nov. 2nd, the 33 year old man was never seen alive again.

Upon finding his bed undisturbed the following morning, Father Benedict Callahan, SJ alerted the Sheriff's office fearing a terrible accident. Many a local volunteer joined the search for the missing priest by scouring the local woods and beaches to no avail. The only traces of his misadventure were his clothing and shoes arranged in an orderly manner on a lonely rock that overlooked the rapid currents of North Beach. Although no body has yet come to shore, Father John O'Malley has been pronounced dead on this grimmest of autumn days.

I re-read the article several times over and two things immediately struck me as extremely odd. The first was that Father O'Malley would choose a November day to go swimming. Even if he was just a guest in town and not acquainted with the ways of the Straits of Juan de Fuca anyone could have told him that it would have been nearly impossible to swim without a wetsuit most times of the year but especially in November. Autumn on the peninsula brought in strong cold currents from Alaska that chased the whales to the South. This left the water so frigid that anyone who was unlucky enough to step into it felt the freezing cold waves like knives on the skin. Why hadn't the priests stopped him?

The second thing that struck me as odd was that November 2, 1953 was the day that Margot gave birth to Deidre and Morgan. All Soul's Day had always been a special day for my family and we had little jokes about the Winships always being born around this particular time of the year. But it seemed strange that while Margot was giving birth, this priest had lost his life in a most uncommon manner.

I set the article aside and pulled out the first of three black covered journals that was dated June 1953 and had the words "Property of Father John O'Malley" written across the top. I opened the first one up and began to read the monk's own words:

June, 20th 1953 –My arrival at the Eisenbeis Monastery

After a long journey here by train and then by bus from the Mother House in San Francisco I was pleasantly surprised to find my quarters quite comfortable and for a moment my mind felt eased. This changed immediately upon meeting Father Benedict. The very second that I held out my hand to greet him the darkness began to swirl inside me like a deep mire. It almost seemed as if he had noticed the subtle change, like the sun moving behind a cloud on a bright day, my inner darkness or what I have come to know as the entity within began to stir. We will start what we have told the others priests are to be my "special classes" but what in reality is the removal of this entity from my soul. I can't seem to remember what it was like not to have it within but there must have been a time when I could think clearly and see the world for its good and not just the abundance of sin that I both loathe and want to partake in. I fear that this is my last chance and that if Father Benedict is unable to help in the banishing of this darkness that is swallowing me I will have no choice but to succumb to the dark deeds that it whispers into my ears constantly. I pray that he may help and that I may be freed of this burden that is becoming more and more difficult to bear.

June 23rd, 1953

The first few days have proved to be helpful in the removal of the entity. Father Benedict has devoted nearly all of his time to helping me with the exception of his daily work in the rose gardens. After his first attempt to exercise the spirit I fell into a sickness that was unexplainable and violent. It shook my body to its root but upon waking I felt a moment of tremendous clarity. There was a tiny pinhole of light that seemed to pierce the darkness and I could almost allow myself the slightest bit of joy. The hope to be able to give Mass again was rekindled. The long lost desire to join my fellow priests with a light heart and a renewal in my faith sat somewhere on the edge of my soul. All of this but a few days earlier had seemed almost impossible. Could it be that Father Benedict will be able to identify and remove this being? He has told me that we must find its name but in the meantime we will slowly remove its grip on my soul and allow my spirit room to battle it instead of being suffocated in its unrelenting grasp. I believe that if anyone can do this he can and that my Guardian angels have not abandoned me after all.

June 25th, 1953
I saw her for the first time today in the rose garden with Father Benedict, like Eve slithering towards Adam with an apple in her hand. She stood there laughing in her obscenely tight dress and protruding midsection which could only mean that she was with child. The voice inside me said that she is a whore and a witch and something that should be destroyed along with the abomination that grows within her. I can't stop the voice now, it chatters away day and night and after I saw her standing so close to Father Benedict while one of the other priests took their picture next to his prize rose, I ran and locked myself in my room and actually vomited up a live toad. What can this mean? I dare not tell Father Benedict as it seems that she has come between us and must be in league with the entity, taunting and flaunting and torturing me. I can't stop thinking about her, that dark hair and the way that she moved so confidently and how Father Benedict listened to her every word as if he was the student and she the teacher. How can this be that my savoir has himself been bewitched?

I heard the door open downstairs and quickly stuffed the journals back in the black envelope along with the other papers and tucked them under my arm. I quickly turned off the light and closed the attic door. As I turned to go back to the turret room I heard the lock click which was most certainly the attic door locking itself behind me. My head was spinning with the discovery of the monk's journals and this piece of Margot's past that I knew nothing about until this moment. Obviously the woman that had so offended the monk had to have been Margot as the identical situation he described was captured in the photo of her and Father Benedict.

"Charlotte?" I heard Deidre's voice call from downstairs as I quickly hid the journals under my mattress and closed my bedroom door.

"I'm up here, I'll be down in a second," I called while leaning over the banister. I could hear my mother Deidre beginning to talk to Margot as they made their way to the kitchen. I took a moment to simply gather my composure before heading to hear news of Morgan. The monk's words were still swirling in my mind and with them a certain feeling of dread had gathered around me as if simply reading about this entity had conjured it to my side. I did what Margot had long ago taught me to do when I felt something around me that I could not control or that was part of the darkness. I grounded my feet, put my hands together and spoke to the house in a whisper filled with power that invited only beings of the highest orders of light into my space and banished anything seeking to harm. Immediately the air felt clear again as if the encroaching darkness had turned tail and ran as I could still feel the waves of purple light still emanating from my body. There were after all some advantages to being a Winship.

CHAPTER 10

Deidre was sitting on the countertop when I entered the kitchen. Her dark hair spilling down past her waist and her hands speckled with little confetti dots of all colors of paint. I wondered when she managed to sleep with running her store in the day, painting into the night and seeing her longtime lover Samir when she had a moment's time. But Deidre was simply one of those people who seemed to have a never ending abundance of energy. It flowed from her in constant rays of yellow and orange that could light up a room if you knew how to watch for an aura. But tonight she looked uncharacteristically tired and pale. I could tell that she had not slept or eaten for far too many hours and was almost to the point of collapsing.

I made my way to her hoping that my presence would ease some of her worry. As we held on to each other I could feel her tired body start to shake as she let out the tears that she had been holding back since Morgan was discovered burnt and on the very edge of death. My mother and I had always been very close but sometimes it felt like we were more like sisters than mother and child. She had me young and my father had died not long after my birth which left her to raise me alone with Margot and George watching over and lending a hand like the parents of us both.

Slowly she regained her composure and slid down from the counter top and moved towards the table by the woodstove. Margot came out of the pantry and set out some of her homemade apple butter and crackers while settling into her chair. I noticed that her alter to the Madonna had been restocked with new candles that were all burning bright and the stove had a new log crackling away. I took my place at the table and realized this was the first time all three of us had been together in three years. With a trembling voice Deidre began to tell us all she knew about Morgan's condition.

"Charlotte, I know that you know some of what has happened so I won't go back over that but there are some things that I just found out. The specialist will be here tonight via helicopter now that the storm has died down," she glanced at Margot who was simply starring at her own folded hands, "but there is something that no one seems to be able to explain. The burns that he has are all over his body and by all accounts he should be dead. They cannot figure out how he is still alive and more so the burns are like nothing they have ever seen. Almost otherworldly is what they keep saying. No one thinks that he will be able to recover but he is still hanging on without any machines, just hydration."

I let the details sink in and the cracking of the fire in the stove punctuated Deidre's words.

"What did Samir say?" I asked, trusting that if anyone would know the details of the situation and would be willing to tell Deidre it would be him. Samir was the closest thing to a father figure, besides my Grandpa George, that I had had growing up. He and Deidre had been together for almost half of my life although they still had their own houses and cringed whenever anyone mentioned the words marriage.

Samir had come to Port Townsend from Seattle where he had been an ER doctor. He had begun to feel the early signs of burn out after working days on end tending to gunshot wounds and all kinds of violence that humans waged against each other's bodies. A small town hospital where the emergencies were of the accidental variety had been his solution for keeping a moniker of sanity. Upon his arrival his first stop had been my Mother's shop "The Curious Crow Antiques." Samir was restoring one of the large Victorian houses that overlooked the bay on his days off from working in the ER at the small Jefferson County Hospital. It was a bit of love at first sight. Deidre swore that she was the one bewitched by his dark eyes, caramel skin and accent that would make more than one local woman swoon. Thankfully, last night he had been the one on call and had tended to Morgan until the specialists could be brought in.

"He has never seen anything like it. Samir said that it is as if the fire burned from the inside out," she said with a choke in her voice. The tea kettle began to whistle and Margot poured each of us one of her herb mixes that was meant to calm and soothe. We sat sipping the warmth in while Deidre explained that the burn specialist would tell us more as soon as he arrived. Samir had pleaded with her to go home to rest while he kept a vigil through the night.

"They have Morgan sealed off in a special room to prevent infections and he is in a coma. I'm sorry for telling you to come for a funeral, Charlotte. I honestly believed that he was dead when I called you. It wasn't a ploy to get you home, I know how happy you are in Seattle with James and far from all the town whispers," she said and I knew that she was being truthful. In all honesty I couldn't have imagined not being home considering the events that had taken place and there was a certain comfort in being at this table with Margot and Deidre. Whenever the three of us were together I could feel a current of energy moving between us that filled in all the empty space.

"We should all get some rest tonight," said Margot as she lifted her eyes from her hands and took a sip of her tea. "I've already told Charlotte but I can feel that something is coming and it is powerful in a way that I do not completely understand. It is coming for Morgan and that means that it will have to go through us first."

I could feel a hush come over the room and couldn't help but think of the proverbial calm before the storm especially when it came to Margot. For a moment I wanted to mention the monk but I couldn't think of how I could tell Margot that I had just broken into her memories and snooped into something that she herself had never read. The horrible words that had been written about her made me queasy with hate and loathing although I still felt compelled to read the rest of what the possessed monk had written. Deep down I knew there was a connection with Morgan although the link still wasn't clear in my mind. So I decided that instead of telling Margot and Deidre about the monk spirit I would at least tell them about "the Strangers."

They listened patiently as I told them about the ghost child's message and the response of the town ghosts to the words "the Strangers." I could only guess that this was the thing that was coming for Morgan.

"I've never heard of anything called 'the Strangers' before," said Deidre. "But the name doesn't sound comforting and if the ghosts are afraid of it that worries me too. They really aren't afraid of much."

Margot sat quietly listening to the house creek as a subtle wind began to stir outside.

"I am sure we will find out soon enough what these beings are and what they want from Morgan," Margot finally said, "but in the meantime it is time to rest. Deidre, I want you to stay here tonight so we can all be together in case something happens at the hospital and also in case these 'Strangers' decide to make a midnight appearance."

So it was agreed that Deidre would sleep in her old room and as I gave them each a long hug and made my way back up to the turret I couldn't help but wonder what was coming and what the monk's tale had to do with it all. There was a phone on every floor of the house and so I thought it was more than time to give James a call and tell him what had transpired but with a quick edit of the more paranormal aspects. When he answered the phone he was livid that it had taken me so long to call him. He had of course been worrying all day long but as I explained the circumstances he calmed and just let me tell him what little I knew of Morgan's condition. I could hear the familiar sounds in the background and it gave me a sudden longing to be with him in Seattle curled up on our couch watching a movie or just talking about our day. But I wasn't ready to let him in on everything there was to know about me just yet because I couldn't help but fear that it would scare him away just when I was becoming so attached. When we finally hung up I knew that he would be appeased for a day or so but that soon I would have to tell him all that was happening in not just "Charlotte's world" but in "Graves' world" as well.

CHAPTER 11

Back in my turret room I managed to find an old pair of pajamas that I had left behind three years earlier -- still folded neatly in the dresser drawer. I switched on the Victorian bedside lamp, climbed into bed and carefully reached under the mattress and grabbed the first of the monk's journals that I had started to read earlier. Part of me felt almost afraid to delve back into this man's mind as the darkness of his thoughts was almost palpable. At first I just held the journal in my hands looking at the cover and preparing myself for what was to be revealed. I knew that there was a reason that I was being shown this and it most certainly had to do with Morgan.

I opened the journal and began to read where I had left off earlier.

June 26, 1953

She comes here every day now to talk to Father Benedict and I can smell her when she is on the grounds. It is a sickening stench of roses wilting and burning and I am both repulsed and drawn to her like a moth to a flame. The entity laughs at me; I can hear its high pitched cackle echo through my brain mimicking the sounds of this Jezebel. I dream about her at night and then wake to punish myself for allowing her to tempt me endlessly. Father Benedict has been trying to help with the removal of the entity but it seems pointless when he himself is obviously a victim of this Winship sorcery that the other priests have told me about. How can he free me when he himself is enslaved by this creature and the seemingly harmless advice that she gives him about the upkeep of the rose garden which I am sure is part of her witchery. Something must be done.

June 27, 1953

I have taken to following her when I can absence myself from the monastery without anyone noticing my being gone. I have seen how her husband dotes on her and the child that she carries and I pity and envy him all at the same time. The entity has told me that he too is bewitched by her and that the only way to free us all is to eliminate her but there is still a part of me that recoils at the thought of physical violence. The entity has tried in vain before for me to commit the worst of sins in breaking the sixth commandment but am I not now guilty of committing the tenth commandment? Do I covet this man's wife? Do I want her for my own or do I simply want to destroy what I cannot have and the object of my desire and torture alike. The entity wants me to think that this is her doing but I am beginning to wonder if it is not my own doing. Father Benedict had become suspicious of my absences and I can tell he is concerned for his flock. Am I the wolf preying on the lamb? Or is she the one who has put rapture on me? I do not know and my mind is more convoluted by the day. I think I must try again to remove this darkness from my soul and put my faith again in Father Benedict that he is indeed God's instrument.

June 30, 1953

A change has again come over me in the past few days after Father Benedict worked tirelessly on the removal of the entity. My body feels bent and broken after the hours of prayer and ritual that have made up my days. After the second day of remaining in the Monastery I began to feel a pain in my stomach and while Father Benedict doused me in holy water and held my shoulders as we prayed I wretched and three iron nails spewed from my mouth. How can this be? Father Benedict quickly locked them in his desk and continued un-phased and I wonder how many people like me he has seen in his fifty years as a priest? I also wonder what I did to let this being control me so and when was the moment that it sought me as its prey or did I invite it in all along? I am no Faustus inviting a demon to take my soul for any type of infernal or carnal knowledge so how did it come to this? I have always been a man of God drawn to his glory and a willing servant to his will and yet I cannot shake this demon from me. Is it God's will that I give in to these horrific longings that the entity continually fuels in me or is it the overpowering of the entity that I must strive to achieve? I admit that I am lost in it all like a man swept out to sea fighting a losing battle with a current too strong to possibly overcome. I only pray that Father Benedict will have the strength to hold me above the rising tide. I have managed to limit my movements from the monastery as not to see the witch and it seems to have helped for the time although when I close my eyes the first thing that I see is *her standing below my bedroom window in the rose garden.*

Somewhere in reading the journals I had slowly begun to drift to sleep, his words weaving a strange picture of events into my dreams. I could see Margot walking with Father Benedict in the rose gardens completely oblivious to this possessed man's obsession with her. Then there was Father O'Malley and the huge dark entity that surrounded him wrapping around him like a cloak and sapping all that was good from him like a giant leech. Then the dream would shift and the monk would become Morgan and back and forth until they became almost two sides of the same coin with the entity hovering over them both. Then somewhere in the dream I was back in my turret room as if I was standing to the side of the bed watching over my sleeping body, the lights still on and the journal open beside me as I slept. But I was not alone in the room, there was a small child's ghost crouched in the corner and she was whispering and rocking back and forth. I couldn't make out her words for there was a loud banging coming from the hallway. But it wasn't the hallway but rather someone was banging from inside the attic door furiously turning the locked doorknob trying to get out. The banging became more frantic and with it the little ghost's whispers grew slowly louder and more urgent until she stood up and screamed "HIDE, they're here!"

I sat straight up in bed awake and aware of the ghost's presence in the room. I could almost hear the faint echo of the banging on the attic door as my mind readjusted to being awake. The house was quiet and as I looked at the clock by my bed it read 3 a.m. exactly. I could feel the cold chill that had settled over the room.

There was an electric feeling in the air and the faint sounds of the bell tower ringing on its own filled the morning hush. As I got up slowly from the bed I asked the small child ghost "who is here?" and she replied in a whisper "the Strangers." I let the words sink in and then made my way over to the window. The fog was still thick in the air and as I looked down from the third story I thought I could make out two figures standing just outside the iron gates that bordered the Winship house.

From above the figures looked tall and thin and while it was hard to make out their features they were each wearing simple dark clothing and Stetson style hats. It was as if they had stepped out of the 1940s and landed here in Port Townsend many a decade too late.

I planted my feet in the usual grounding position and began to gather my energy. Focusing on them I spoke out loud and said "Only beings of the highest orders of light are allowed into my space and I banish anything seeking to harm!" With a crackle of electricity both of the figures jerked their heads up to look at me in one synchronized movement. A smile spread across their pale faces. Their features were cold looking and their skin was almost a translucent white. Even from this distance I could see little flames moving in the whites of their eyes. And above all else I felt power emanating from them like nothing I had ever experienced before from anything or anyplace. In a flash, Margot and Deidre were at my side. They peered down at the figures in the fog without speaking. The two creatures gave us a courteous nod and turned to walk back into the deepening mists.

We all knew it was a temporary retreat and that this was just the beginning. Of what we weren't sure but the bell in the old tower was ringing more fervently to signal a ghostly emergency. Without speaking we all left my room and made our ways to our respective corners of the house to begin setting up protection. Margot began to burn sprigs of rue and light her candles in each room while I set special rocks in the four main floor corners of the house. Deidre called on all the birds to guard the eves and the windows. The house began to feel secure if only for the time being and soon we made our way back to our beds knowing that there was nothing more to be done for the night but that the morning light would be here only too soon and that "the Strangers" had now arrived.

When I reached my room I felt the child ghost's presence had gone and then I noticed that the monk's journal was no longer on my bed. I looked under the mattress and there it was tucked beneath with the other two along with the black envelope. Had the ghost spirit hidden it so Margot wouldn't see when she came to my side to meet "the Strangers?" I know that I had left it in plain sight having been startled awake with the second round of haunted dreams in less than 24 hours. Whatever had transpired, the journals would be staying under the mattress until I had gotten at least a tiny bit of sleep. I whispered to the room "Fox, come watch over me." And in a flash the smell of cloves and fresh cut wood was in the room and I felt like I could close my eyes at last with my guardian ghost keeping a lookout over me while I slept like the dead.

CHAPTER 12

The morning came in a flash. If it hadn't been for the banging of pots and pans in the kitchen I would have probably slept until well into the afternoon. Deidre was an early bird and I could smell the earthy scent of coffee and frying bacon wafting up the banister to my room. I let myself enjoy the warmth of the blankets and the familiar perfumes of the Winship house while trying not to think about the journals that were tucked beneath me. Instead the terrifying faces of the mysterious "Strangers" that had made an unusual introduction at the house in the wee hours were in the forefront of my mind. Eventually I flung the covers back and made my way downstairs still in my pajamas and probably with my hair sticking up in all kinds of directions.

Margot was already up and tending to the wood stove. Deidre was pouring three cups of coffee while frying up bacon and eggs in an old cast iron pan that most likely dated back to when the Winship house was built. I ambled into the room and headed straight for my cup of coffee and gave Deidre and Margot quick hugs before settling into my chair, my feet folded under me, close to the warmth of the stove.

"Charlotte," said Margot while sorting through a little stack of her handwritten notes, "can you bring a few things out to Annie Christy this morning? I want to go straight to the hospital but I promised her I would stop by today."

"Of course, I'll take them over now and then meet you and Deidre at the hospital," I said, almost relieved that I had a little more time before I had to actually see the physical damage that the fire had wrecked upon Morgan. A quick shower and a drive out to North Beach would do me good.

Annie Christy was one of Port Townsend's living legends. Her home was deep in the woods by North Beach only a few miles farther down the road from Morgan's Cider Mill. Although when she had built her own house out of logs and cast off iron there had been nothing for at least 15 miles around. Annie Christy was well over a hundred years old and she still lived on her own with no electricity in a house that was patch-worked together next to the most magnificent cactus garden that I had ever seen. She had been my Great-Grandmother Elsiba Winship's dearest friend so I had spent many of my childhood afternoons playing with the prickly plants that grew out of old boots and wagon wheels.

Up until just a few years earlier she would drive herself into town in her very own Ford Model T, turning the crank herself and steering her way up the hill to Margot's house for a weekly visit. But slowly the ravages of time had begun to take their toll on Annie Christy and she was less inclined to leave her forest home. Margot had been asking her to move into the Winship house ever since George had passed away. She always politely refused unwilling to leave her most magnificent garden creation. So it was a bit of a treat to be able to take her a few supplies while visiting with her in the magical place that was her home.

Deidre set three plates on the table and we all sat eating in a silence thick with fatigue and worry until Margot finally mentioned what we were all thinking.

"I guess we will just have to wait and see what these 'Strangers' want from us," she said in a firm voice. "Their power was unlike anything I have ever felt before and I am sure that the charms we put on the house would have been useless against them if they had really wanted to come in."

"I kept feeling the most unsettling mix of cold and heat radiating from them almost like a white hot ember or the kind of burn that comes from having hot skin touch a block of ice," said Deidre while pushing her egg around her plate.

"Did you notice that there were flames in the whites of their eyes," I said, feeling shaky just saying the observations I had made out loud. I couldn't help but think about all that I had read last night in Father O'Malley's journals regarding his possession by an unnamed dark entity. I had learned early in life that all things are revealed at certain times for a reason which made it even more unnerving to think that these "Strangers" arrived the same night that I learned of the obsessions of the priest and the secret link to my family. It could not just be a coincidence but now came the hard part of unraveling the connections that this all had to Morgan. There was surely a thread that wove them all together.

"I am positive we will know more soon enough," said Margot "so for now let's tend to Morgan. Charlotte there are several bags in the mudroom that you can take to Annie and then we will see you at the hospital." And with that Margot put her dishes in the sink and went back to busying herself with all the tasks that she had most likely abandoned yesterday in the shock of what had happened to Morgan. Deidre just gave me a weary look and put her dish in the sink as well and threw on her down coat over her paint clothes. She gave me a hug and a kiss and was on her way to her house and then the hospital as well.

Before I knew it I too was out of the house, dressed and packing the ten sacks of supplies into my trunk to take to Annie. The early morning was filled with a light frost that had settled on the grass. The fog was all but gone and in its place streaking rays of sun were peeking through the grey cloud cover trying in earnest to add a bit of warmth to the autumn air. I made my way down the hill that led out of town towards North Beach. As I turned onto the long stretch of road that led to the lagoons I couldn't help but think of one of our local jokes for giving directions to this part of town. Deidre would wickedly tell tourists that the way to North Beach was to turn right at the cow and left at the red barn which described just about every other house in this part of town. After driving for about ten minutes down the quiet stretch of rural highway there was the familiar bend in the road. To my right lay the lagoons where all the blue herons would congregate and to my left Gavin's childhood home.

He was raised by his Great Aunt and when she had passed he had kept the old cedar farm house with the sad looking stables in the back and the two ancient horses that huddled together inside during the winter snows. But as I passed by I almost ran my car into the ditch I was so surprised to see the state of the old house after being away for three years. The cedar siding and roof had all been replaced and was cleaned of all the moss and decay. There was a new gravel driveway where the dirt road with the many potholes had been. Where the stables had once stood there was now a magnificent red barn. I couldn't help but feel a sense of pride in my dear friend and all that he had built in the few years since I had been in Seattle. It was with a bit of longing that I continued driving past the house and the lagoons.

Soon the old cemetery came into view and the familiar turn into the short driveway that was Morgan's home appeared on my left. I willed myself not to look as I drove by not wanting to see the charred remains of his home and the abandoned Cider Mill. Soon I would have to see his devastated body and the correlation between the burnt beams of his home and his own scorched limbs was too close for me to face just yet. So through the forest road I sped as the trees became denser and the houses spaced farther and farther apart. Through the trees on the right one could catch glimpses of the rolling surf on the often abandoned North Beach.

One of my fondest memories from childhood was after a ravishing autumn storm would roll through the Peninsula; Morgan would come knocking on Deidre's door before dawn. The three of us would head over to North Beach together to comb the sands for unveiled treasures. The storms that hit the coast were more than just a little wind and rain; they had been known to dislodge sunken ships from the watery deeps spitting them onto shore after a hundred years of being lost at sea. So as the winds would rattle my windows and howl through the chimneys I could barely sleep with anticipation of what lost items would soon be thrust upon the sandy beaches waiting for me to find them. With flashlights, windbreakers and tall rubber boots we would explore the low tides when the dangerous ocean waves were at a safe distance and we could comb the sand flats for all kinds of unusual detritus.

A favorite of Deidre's were the hundred year old glass Japanese fishing floats that we would sometimes find by the dozen in all different colors and sizes after a good storm. She would dry the twisted ropes that encircled them and clean the barnacles off the blown glass globes to then hang them all over the wooden shiplap ceiling in her antique shop. We had stopped counting when she had reached a hundred and while she sold some of them to collectors, the best ones had become part of her permanent store decorations.

Morgan on the other hand loved blue glass medicine bottles and it was always surprising how many would wash up on shore still intact and some with a bit of the paper labels attached. He put them in all the windows of his cottage and had little shelves lined with cobalt, aqua blue, amber yellow, olive green and sometimes amethyst-purple glass vessels that created a beautiful light when the sun was shining through them. It almost looked like a cross between an apothecary's cupboard and a stained glass window worthy of a French Cathedral when he lit tiny candles inside of them in the evening.

And while I would also gather all the floats and bottles that I found for my mother and Morgan, dropping them into my old wicker fishing basket, I hunted for unusual rocks and shells that had a naturally worn hole somewhere in them. This may have been the first sign that I would someday become a jewelry designer, since finding a jewel with a hole made attaching stones much easier, but there was also a power that I could feel while holding these elements. A shell with a hole worn into it and smoothed over from swirling in sand and sea was perfect for making a talisman for travel. A white stone with black stripes and a hole through its middle was ideal for identifying a liar in one's midst. Each stone had its power and it seemed that my Winship gift was listening to what magic these earth bound elements whispered to me in their own special way. And this was as true for smoothed down stones and shells as much as for the earth bound spirits that woke me at night to tell me their fears and longings.

Margot had given me her old mason jars that she no longer used for making her cherry and rose preserves and I had slowly filled them with the ocean gifts that had washed up on our shores. I had them organized by their intended power and had labeled them with little tags that read "travel," "love," "hope" and all the human emotions and activities in-between. There was a special jar that I often kept in the very back of my work bench drawer that I knew could be used for darker deeds like manipulating someone's vision of yourself, curse stones and other unsavory longings. I wasn't sure why I kept them other than to remove them from others unsuspecting paths. Deidre warned me that all Winships at one time or another where tempted to use their gifts for ill and having the tools to do so could be dangerous. I kept them all the same, hidden away while I used my other sacred stones to create talismans in a harmony that even the most skeptical often reported back unusually prosperous happenings once receiving the objects I had created.

As I turned down the long dirt road that led deeper into the forest towards Annie's house, I longed for those simple days of beach combing after a storm when everyone was safe and the fires that haunted Morgan had been a thing of the past. To think that just one day before, the monk spirit had simply been one of the many present specters that haunted at a distance and I had never heard the word "the Strangers" whispered on frightened ghost lips.

CHAPTER 13

As I pulled up to the house I could see the Model T parked under a homemade carport that I imagined Annie had erected sometime in the last twenty years. I parked to the side of the expansive fence that bordered her cactus garden. To get to Annie's house one first had to find the latch on her elaborate maze of fencing and the hidden lock that held the gate shut. The gate and fence itself were made with the most unusual scraps of wrought iron, beach wood that was twisted into serpent like shapes, old horseshoes, beach glass, iron keys and even the occasional rusted gear or car part all woven together. She had spent eighty years creating a labyrinth of fencing that enclosed her precious cacti and the house at its center with the chicken coop off to the back and several well behaved goats for milk and cheese.

I quickly found the familiar little knob and latch that released the spring on the gate and popped it open so I could make my way to the house. The sound of wind chimes made from metal, bells and other found objects clinked in the breeze. It was an odd sound that both called me to it in its familiar melody and also left me feeling like I had stepped into a fairy ring and was now lost in a parallel world.

Annie Christy had come to Port Townsend with her brother in the early 1900s and had immediately taken to frontier life. She split her own wood and lined the side of her log cabin with enough to last through even the hardest winters, she trapped animals for meat and in addition to her cactus garden she grew much of her own food. But the rumor around town was that she and her brother were the heirs to one of the large railroad barons that had made their way across the country. She never spoke of her family name and to everyone she was just Annie Christy who certainly was an eccentric especially in her time. She never married and while her brother Evan was a bit of a ladies man around town and lived a drastically different lifestyle than his sister they remained devoted siblings to the end.

The first time I had been inside Annie Christy's house was

when I was a young child and the sparse living conditions had fascinated me. It had been quite the opposite of all the Victorian fuss and intricacy everywhere else in town. There was a large open room that served as her kitchen, bedroom, and living quarters while off to the side of the house through a solid wood door was a room that had been originally destined to be a bedroom. When I was allowed to see inside for the first time my eyes had filled with tears at the mystery and beauty of what I beheld. The windows in this room were covered in newspaper to keep out the light as not to damage any of the room's contents. The walls were lined with curio cabinets that were filled with all of Annie's treasures which included old photos in the most exquisite of frames, gold and gem encrusted eggs, glass perfume bottles from Paris, ornately bound leather books, bronze statues and all types of finery that one would never expect to discover in a humble log cabin. The center of the room of treasures held a long oak table with one chair where I imagined Annie sat at night speaking to the perfume bottles as if they were her children and reading the eggs bedtime stories before tucking them in to sleep.

The thing that I loved most about Annie was that she was one of the few people in town who was not afraid of my gift or any of the Winship women for that matter. In a way she was one of us, using the magic that she found in the natural world to create a safe haven and a life lived with meaning although unconventional to most. I followed the mosaic walkway up to the front porch of the cabin and as my foot hit the first step I noticed Annie sitting still in her outdoor rocking chair with a large blanket over her legs and eyes closed in sleep. I reached over and lightly placed my hand on hers. As her eyes opened, still confused with sleep, I could see that her once clear green eyes had become clouded over with white cataracts.

"Annie, it's me Charlotte," I said softly.

"I thought for a minute you were Elsiba with that long dark hair of yours," she said while slowly rising from her rocker to give me a squeeze. I was always amazed at the strength that Annie contained in such a small and ancient body. How she managed to live here on her own all these years without complaint or illness was beyond me but I only thanked the forest that it took care of her as well as it did.

"Margot sent me out to bring you some supplies and I also wanted to visit while I am here for awhile," I said, not wanting to alarm her with news of what had happened to Morgan. I figured that Margot would be coming to visit later and would give her the details. Annie seemed perfectly happy with my explanation of why I was there. I unloaded all the bags into her house and helped her sort and organize. That was when I realized just how bad her eyesight had become and how she overcame it by creating a system in her cupboards that helped her find things easily. After we had put everything away we sat down for tea at her wooden table for two and I told her about Seattle and James and then almost without thinking I decided to ask Annie what she knew, if anything, about the monk.

"Annie, I was wondering if you remember a priest named Father O'Malley that drowned at North Beach in 1953?" I asked tentatively. Annie was quiet for a moment as if trying to make her way back through time but struggling to keep the thread of present and past from becoming a tangle of events.

"I remember that in 1953 Elsiba was still alive and Margot had your mother and Morgan. There was a fire at the monastery that summer and then the drowning of the priest later that fall. But Charlotte, you have to remember that back then the monks stayed very much to themselves. I do know that his clothing was found just on the other side of my property going down to the beach which was odd because I had checked the beach as soon as I had heard he was missing and had found nothing. Then two days later his clothes were there."

I let her words sink in and then worked up the courage to ask what I was really interested in finding out.

"Did Margot ever say anything about him?" I asked, feeling a wave of guilt come over me that I was again snooping behind my grandmother's back about a past she obviously wanted to forget.

"Well, back then Margot spent a lot of time helping the church with everything from their rose garden to organizing the Sunday school activities and all the fundraisers and events in-between. Elsiba was never much for that kind of thing but it was dear to Margot so she allowed it and since she and George were expecting it seemed harmless enough. But I do remember hearing talk around town that Father

O'Malley had distaste for the Winships. Honestly dear, it was so long ago that things have become a little hazy. Just last night I could have sworn that I saw two men in Stetson hats standing by my back door looking in the window at me but when I looked back nothing was there."

I felt a shiver run through my body. "The Strangers" had come here last night as well although I couldn't for the life of me think what they would want with old Annie Christy. A sudden need to protect her came over me and in my mind I sent out light to all corners of her home to keep anything unwanted away from Annie. I looked down at my watch and realized that the morning had flown by in a hurry and it was time that I head to the hospital. I helped Annie with a few more things around her house all the time worrying about why "the Strangers" had been lurking around the outside of her back door at night staring in her windows. It not only left me feeling terrified but it also angered me that whatever these creatures were they would prey on a helpless almost blind old woman. I held her in my arms a little longer when I left and asked her if she didn't want to stay with us in the Winship house instead of all alone out in the woods. She declined as always stating that her cacti needed her. I whispered a final protection spell as I closed her gate behind me and waved to her while getting in the car. She went back to rocking in her chair with her blanket draped over her legs and the wind chimes singing their forlorn tune.

CHAPTER 14

Like most people, hospitals are not a place that I care to visit. In the corridors the final wishes of the sick and dying are too present for someone like me who can feel it behind every door and drawn curtain. If it was only the living and their prayers for healing and miracles, I wouldn't mind the hospital as much but there were other things that lingered in the shadows. I called them sickness demons. They are drawn to these places for the suffering and the decay. Squatting in corners to help spread infection, disease and pain wherever they go thus thriving on the consequences of their wicked deeds.

When I made my way through the automatic doors at Jefferson County Hospital I could feel them scatter as the smell of disinfectant wafted into my nostrils. I tried to ignore their presence and just focus on getting to Morgan's room without being overwhelmed by the ongoing tragedy that a hospital contains. Nurses bustled by with trays of pills. Doctors rushed from room to room with their clipboards and stethoscopes in hand convinced that they can cheat death again and again.

As I was rounding the corner which led to the intensive care unit I stopped dead in my tracks. Two tall pale figures were standing motionless peering into one of the hospital rooms. I quickly ducked behind a wall and slowly peeked around the edge to make sure that these figure were indeed "the Strangers." They stood perfectly still side by side with long dark coats and Stetson hats perched on their hairless heads. With the overhead florescent lights in the hospital their white skin looked even more translucent. The other thing that immediately caught my attention was that people were bustling around them completely oblivious to their presence. I saw one nurse step around the pair without looking and continued on her way down the hall. A small boy rounded the corner with his mother and started pointing at them and tugging her pant leg to get her attention. She stopped and let the boy whisper in her ear while he continued to point furiously at the enigmatic men in hats. But the mother just shook her head as she looked directly at them but saw nothing. The two men ignored the child and kept staring into the hospital room until a heart monitor went off and several nurses and doctors made a dash into the very room "the Strangers" were hovering near.

A commotion ensued as a crash cart was rolled into the room while "the Strangers" watched motionless. In a frantic bustle the healthcare workers did their best to resuscitate the poor soul whose heart had stopped beating. This went on for several minutes while I stayed in my hiding place until I finally heard the heart monitor switch off. When I looked back around the corner "the Strangers" were gone and I heard a doctor say to the nurse as he left the room that someone needed to notify the family.

My heart was thudding in my chest as I sprinted from my hiding place. I crept down the hall fearful of coming face to face with "the Strangers." A quick glance into the room where the heart monitor went off revealed the empty shell of a body covered in a hospital death shroud. The white sheet lay over the corpse as the machines were slowly detached by the remaining nurse. The sense of terror that rushed through me was almost overwhelming coupled with the usual hospital demons and I thought for a second that I might pass out. I hurried down the hallway as fast as I could without breaking into a full run while a rising sense of panic washed over me. Did "the Strangers" somehow precipitate this faceless person's death? Why could only some people see them and not others? All these thoughts were flooding through my mind as well as the obvious fear that my family was somehow a target as well for these mysterious and terrifying creatures. As I rounded the corner I ran straight into Samir almost knocking him over as he grabbed my shoulders to steady himself. I barely managed to stifle a scream and he kept holding my shoulders even after he had regained his footing.

"Wow, Charlotte. Are you ok?" he said as I began to tremble. I just nodded quickly, afraid to open my mouth for fear of crying, screaming or both. He hugged me and tried to comfort me as I finally let myself succumb to tears. They streaked down my cheeks for the first time since I had heard about Morgan's condition and I just let it all come pouring out.

"Don't worry Charlotte, we are doing all that we can for Morgan and your Mom and Margot are with him right now," he said, doing his best to try to calm me down. His years of being an ER physician gave him an almost preternatural sense of calm in the face of adversity. Of course I couldn't tell him about what I had just seen transpire only steps from where we stood. After a few minutes I slowly began to regain my composure as Samir led me to Morgan's room.

"I shouldn't have to tell you not to run in the halls," Samir said with a little smirk as we approached a sealed off room with an observation window where Margot and Deidre stood watch. I was sure that my eyes were puffy and red but no one said anything as I looked through the window into Morgan's room. I couldn't help but feel shock at seeing the strange burns that covered most of his body. Dark swirls covered his skin and while it was obvious that the marks were burns it was unlike anything I had ever seen. Some parts where almost black but throughout there was a strange pattern like scales that undulated from his face down to his toes. The half of Morgan's face that was visible to us was untouched which gave me a small sense of relief that I could recognize a part of the man still in existence beneath what was left of his tortured skin.

"The specialist said that he has never seen a burn quite like this before and there is really no explanation for why he is still alive," said Margot. "They are still hydrating him for the time being and trying to avoid any infections by keeping him sealed off in this room. So basically we don't know anything more than we did a few hours ago." I could hear the growing frustration in her voice as she spoke about the doctor's prognosis for Morgan's recovery which was slim to none.

"Is he in pain?" I asked, not entirely wanting to know the answer.

"They don't think so since he is in a coma," said Deidre, "All I feel from him is a sort of drifting feeling, like he is not entirely in his body."

"We are going to go home for a while since they will not let us get any closer than this for the time being and Deidre needs to open her store," said Margot as she starred longingly through the window.

As soon as Samir had hurried off for his rounds I whispered to Margot and Deidre, "The Strangers were just here." I explained all that I had just seen as the color drained from their faces and then continued on to tell them about Annie Christy having seen them at her house during the night.

"I will try to talk Annie into coming to the Winship house," said Margot, "and in the meantime I think someone should stay here with Morgan until we know more about these 'Strangers.' I don't want Morgan here helpless, not that I would know what to do to fend these beings off if they chose to attack us."

"I will stay and keep the first watch," I said. Margot and Deidre agreed and we set up an impromptu schedule to keep in order that someone was always there to watch over Morgan in case "the Strangers" or anything else tried to harm him. After they left I settled into a folding chair by the door where I could periodically look in on Morgan through the window while still resting my tired body. Even though I despised being in this place I could not shake the image of "the Strangers" peering into the room of a helpless soul and I refused to let the same thing happen to Morgan.

For several hours I sat listening to the sounds of the hospital and the scuttling of dark creatures from under gurneys and behind doorways. Samir brought me a cup of bad coffee to hold me over until Margot could come to take the next shift. As I stretched my legs and looked in on Morgan I could feel a sudden shift in the air around me. The hallway became quiet and I began to feel the familiar presence that I had come to associate with Morgan early on in my life. It was almost as if the darkness that clung to him was hovering above his bed like a black cloud, expanding and contracting with his every breath. For a moment I caught the faint familiar smell of burnt hair. I leaned in closer to the window that separated us to try to see if I could make any sense of the burn pattern on his arm.

The burn lines were like hideous waves that had scorched his flesh as they moved over his body. It was hard to imagine how something like this had come to pass. Morgan was only a few feet on the other side of the glass so I could almost make out symmetry to the burn pattern that repeated as it moved across his skin. I followed it up his arm to his shoulder and then to his chin when I realized that his head was no longer looking up at the ceiling but was rather facing me. The right side of his face was covered with the swirling burns and his right eye looked like it was melted shut. As I scanned over his face it took me several seconds to realize that his left eye was open and staring at me. In it I could see a pain so deep that it seared through me like a hot knife. I could feel that the darkness that usually enveloped Morgan was hovering over me as well. My eyes were riveted to his one wide open, unblinking left eye. It had fixed me in a gaze that left me frozen in place.

Suddenly he screamed "Malek!" I was so startled that I jumped from my chair and dropped my coffee cup on the floor. When I looked back up he was back to facing the ceiling with his eye closed as if nothing had happened. I could hear the one word ringing in my ears as one of the orderlies kindly rushed to help me clean the spilled liquid from around my feet. Chills were running down my spine as the dark presence retreated back into Morgan's body. I began to mutter a prayer under my breath to keep the other dark beings in the hospital away as well as the beings of light to help me make sense of yet another clue in this deepening mystery. It was all too clear that Morgan's life was what hung in the balance.

CHAPTER 15

It was hard not to run out of the hospital when Margot came back to take over the next shift of watching over Morgan. I kept the incident of his sudden awakening and shouting of the word "Malek" to myself. My suspicion was deepening to the link between Morgan and Father O'Malley and I couldn't think of a way to even begin that conversation with Margot. Moving through the hallways out to the front door I could hardly wait to find a place to read the rest of Father O'Malley's journal. The cool afternoon air hit my face and gave me a new surge of life as I was finally liberated from the hospital or what I liked to call the prison for the sick and dying.

Making my way back into town I noticed several new cafes had opened since I had left. It looked as if the town youth finally had a place to congregate other than that post office steps. Despite the allure of the new hangouts with their overstuffed couches, there was only one place I wanted to go where I could read the journals in peace. Before leaving the house I had wrapped an old book sleeve that I had found in the Winship house library around the journal and tucked it into my purse to read later. I turned off to park on the side street by the Palace Hotel which was formerly one of the many town brothels in the early 1900s. It was now a towering red brick inn with rooms named after the working girls of old. On the backside of the building with the bell tower looming on the cliffs above, I saw the familiar sign swaying in the wind that read "Gunn Grocery and Café."

Tobias Gunn had opened his grocery store in 1946 after coming home from fighting in WWII with a permanent limp in his right leg and a war weary heart. He and my Grandfather George had been fast friends and for as long as I could remember the two of them could always be found playing cards and eating peanuts in Tobias' store on Sunday afternoons. Up until a few years ago he was the only grocery store for miles around. And while he was well into his 80's he kept his door open for all of the locals, like Margot, who refused to shop at the chain stores. One side of the old-fashioned shop was lined with rows of canned goods while the center had a long wooden table filled with crates of fresh fruits and vegetables from the local farms. On the other side of the store was a traditional espresso machine, an antique pastry case filled with delicacies and several small café tables lined up against the windows. Tobias had fallen in love with Paris when he had marched through its streets during the Liberation and from then on he carried a bit of nostalgia for the European bistros.

Tobias Gunn was one of those rare men that wore their heart on their sleeve. During the mill workers strike in the 1970s he carried all the mill families in groceries for almost 8 months making sure that half the town stayed fed while they fought for better pay and safer working conditions. Even to this day he gave groceries on credit the old fashioned way where he wrote down people's names on little index cards and kept a running tally that they could pay at the end of the month.

I pushed open the old wooden door and heard the familiar ring of the bell that was fastened tightly to the weary hinge. Old Tobias came hobbling out of the backroom and gave a spry little jump of happiness when he saw me setting my bag down at one of his tables.

"Well hello Miss Charlotte!" he said enthusiastically as he smiled wide, "I almost thought you would never come back to us!" The liver spots on his balding head had nearly taken over the entire surface of skin. His hands were so gnarled with age and arthritis that it hardly seemed right for him to be making me a cup of coffee.

"You know I could never stay away from you for too long," I said while settling down at the café table. This was the one place where I could read without interruption. As he steamed the milk and poured me my favorite of his concoctions I removed the journal with its new cover claiming that it was a book of 19th century English poetry. We chatted for a bit about Seattle life and I told him about my jewelry business and the small house that James and I shared until a little flurry of customers came in that needed tending to. Tobias helped them pick out the perfect autumn squash. As I watched him shake and tap on the gourds testing for freshness, I noticed in the doorway that led to the backroom a woman watching me. I had all but forgotten about his wife

June who had passed away almost twenty years earlier. There she was watching her husband with a sadness that was palpable.

She knew that I could see her but she just stood motionless and whispered, "I'm waiting," and turned on her heel and went into the backroom. Waiting for Tobias is what I was sure she meant. I could only hope that her wait would continue a good while longer as the world needed men like him to add a little sweetness to the darkness that seemed more pervasive.

I tentatively opened the monk's journal to where I had left off just last night and with a feeling of dread and curiosity I began to read his haunting words.

July 1st, 1953

It seems like everyone in this town has a heathen-like infatuation with their Fourth of July parade and fireworks ceremony and I am sure that this excuse for revelry will be nothing more than a disguised maypole celebration a few months too late. The entity has been quiet the past few days and Father Benedict has asked me to help with the preparations for some sort of refreshment stand that the monks have each year. I will have to oblige him as he has dedicated so much of his time to my "special classes" but I dread this type of festivity as I am sure that Margot Winship will be in attendance and I know that the minute I see her, the darkness will come. Two days ago Father Benedict managed to get the first letter of the entities name and it was an "M." He was unable to get the demon to speak more than a simple letter and it was clear that the beast gave up the one syllable in taunting rather than in revealing anything. I spent two days after that moment cloistered in my room repeating this prayer day and night:

Lord, almighty, merciful and omnipotent God,

Father, Son and Holy Spirit,

Drive out from me all influence of evil spirits.

Father, in the name of Christ,

I plead you to break any chain that the devil has on me.

Pour upon me the most precious blood of your Son.

May His immaculate and redeeming blood break all bonds of my body or mind.

I ask you this through the intercession of the Most Holy Virgin Mary.

Archangel St. Michael, intercede and come to my help.
In the name of Jesus I command all devils that could have any influence over me,
To leave me forever.
By His scourging,
His crown of thorns,
His cross,
By His blood and Resurrection,
I command all evil spirits to leave me.
By the True God
By the Holy God
By God who can do all,
I command you, filthy demon, to leave me in the name of Jesus, my Savior and Lord.

I hold this prayer in my mind and on my lips in each moment and I can only pray that I can be strong and hold the entity at bay while I bear the witch's presence.

July 2nd, 1953

The entity has begun to stir as we get closer to the celebration and I can feel its grip tightening on my stomach and my loins. It seems that there are holes in my days that I cannot account for and Father Benedict fears that the entity has begun to take over for hours at a time. I fear for the safety of others and have asked to remain at the monastery during the parade and town picnic but he insists that the entity wants me to be isolated so it can get a firmer hold on me. No more progress has been made to obtain its name and so I continue with my prayer that has turned into an almost constant muttering of the chant under my breath. And still mixed in with my revulsion and attraction is the image of Margot Winship, wife and expecting mother and filthy dirty conniving maligning whore of a witch. She is all I think about and in ways that sicken me and yet I cannot stop the pictures that flash through my mind of horrific violence that the entity assures me will free me once and for all.

I have hinted at this to Father Benedict and he tells me endlessly that this woman is a good Catholic who has a gift from God and should be admired and I am astounded that he cannot see her for what she really is. Even the other women in town talk about how she has a power that you can feel and that she has used it to seduce her unwitting husband and to manipulate the minds of the men folk. Her mother is the same and more than once have I seen this Elsiba Winship turning the heads of the young men in town as she rides around in an old Model T with a strange old crone who lives alone in the woods. I imagine the three of them dancing nude in a witches Sabbath of the hag, the mother, the maiden mocking the priests and twisting the minds of the innocent. I must destroy her and the child that she will bear before it can wreak havoc on the earth.

July 5th, 1953

I refused to go to the 4th of July parade and instead locked myself in my room until the priests eventually left me to rot in the dank cellar that inhabits my mind. I am not sure whether or not I should thank Father Benedict for returning to check on me or curse him for letting me live but at some moment while I was in my room I must have lost time again and when I woke the room was filled with flames. They licked the plaster off the stone walls and in them I could see the face of the entity beckoning me to join it in hell as I crawled across the floor in the smoke filled room. Two of the priests and Father Benedict were able to break down the locked wooden door and pull me from the inferno that had nearly consumed the room and was moving its way up the north tower. By the time the volunteer fire department heard the ringing of the bell tower and got to the castle the entire tower was engulfed in flames and it is only by a miracle that I escaped and with me this journal that I keep in my robes at all times.

Slowly the town gathered around the monastery as the men fought to stop the flames and it was as if the demonic blaze had become the town's own twisted version of a fireworks display. As I lay gasping while the town doctor was preparing to transport me to the small hospital I saw Margot staring at me with what I almost thought was a smirk. Her husband was one of the fire fighters and while her stare was focused on him almost the entire time that little smirk gave me a firm reason to think that maybe she was the cause of the fire and not the entity. Did she know that I lusted after her and loathed her all at the same time? Was it I who was the victim all along and she not the innocent lamb but the lion with eyes lit up by flames?

I looked up as I was about to turn the page and noticed for the first time that the sky had begun to darken although it was only 3 p.m.

in the afternoon. A slight wind had begun to whistle into the little cracks under the windowsill. I caught sight of a group of crows flying low to the ground, which was a sure sign of a heavy rain to come. Letting the monk's words sink in I felt my own protectiveness for my family begin to stir. Whatever this entity was it had a torturous hold on this man. It had warped his perceptions into what I was sure would become complete madness. Only a very strong person could overcome what was inside of him and I couldn't help but be reminded of the series of fires that had followed Morgan since childhood the first of which was coincidentally at the Fourth of July picnic in 1960.

The story that I had always heard whispered by townsfolk was that when Morgan and Deidre were just six years old they went with Margot and George and the rest of the town to Chetzemoka Park for the picnic after the big Independence Day parade. A group of older children had been playing in the rose arbors. When Morgan and Deidre had wanted to pass through the arches filled with the blossoms to get to the small bridge on the other side an older boy had pushed Deidre into one of the bushes. When Morgan saw his sister with blood running down her forehead and streaks of crimson all over her arms and dress, a fire had spontaneously engulfed not only the clothing of the offending boy but the entire rose arbor. The boy was lucky that he remembered to quickly roll on the grass to put out the fire but the rose bushes weren't as mobile and it had taken the whole town to put out the blaze.

I felt an odd little tap on my shoulder and thinking it was Tobias turned my head. Instead I came nose to nose with a young boy of the familiar grey color that I associated with the dead. His clothing was from the early sixties and he must have been about ten or eleven when he had died. I immediately identified him as being Tobias and June's late son Hugo. He had died of a fever and I had seen him from time to time in the café standing near the unsuspecting Tobias or occasionally mischievously knocking over cans when a tourist got too close. But today his eyes were filled with fear as he leaned in and whispered in my ear, "Don't let the Strangers take us, Charlotte."

A loud crack filled the room as something hit the window next to me. In a flash I could feel Hugo's presence flee the room as I turned to see what had made the noise. On the ground just outside the window lay a dead crow. It doesn't take a witch to know that a dead bird is a bad omen. Although what was really bothering me were Hugo's words and the ever deepening suspicion that the link between Father O'Malley and Morgan had fire as the key.

CHAPTER 16

It took me until it was closing time to finish the last pages of Father O'Malley's first journal. His deepening struggles had continued through the summer of 1953. He would vacillate between thinking that Margot was the source of his possession into moments of lucidity when he knew that the entity was manipulating and controlling him. He spoke of the rebuilding of the burnt tower as a sign of his redemption as he worked with the monks to construct a new wing where his old room had been devoured by a demonic fire. But as I reached the last few pages the ravings became increasingly violent and his obsessions with Margot were both shocking and terrifying for my sheltered eyes.

Tobias gave me a hug and made me promise to stop by everyday while I was in town which I was sure I would be doing whether he wanted me to or not so I could finish the journals without fear of discovery. As I wrapped my scarf around my neck three times and flipped my hood up to shelter my head from the rain I noticed that the dead crow was gone from outside the window and the rain was beginning to beat down on the town with a growing intensity. It was only a quick walk to Deidre's shop although she had probably closed by now and was heading back to the hospital as per our schedule. Not wanting to go back to the Winship house I made my way to the Waterside Brewery to see Kat and Gavin in the hopes that I could clear my mind of the darkness that had seeped in while reading Father O'Malley's words.

I began to feel cleansed as I walked the six blocks east. Looking up into the uninhabited portions of the many buildings that lined downtown I could see the familiar ghostly faces staring back at me, unmoving. As I passed the Rose Theatre, I felt the familiar chill of a ghost trying to get my attention. Glancing across the street from under the hood of my jacket two grey men were standing motionless under the theatre marquis. One made a beckoning motion with his finger for me to come over while the other remained still. I felt a growing dread looking on the two of them. I put my hand out and in my mind told them to stay away but instead they began to follow me down the street. I picked up my pace and then suddenly the two ghosts were standing in front of me blocking my path. Gathering all my power within I stood my ground I asked them "What do you want?"

"You know what we want," the vocal one said while the other just stared impassively. That was when I realized that these two were probably on what I called a loop. They were repeating the steps that led to their death as either a type of self-inflicted purgatory or out of sheer incomprehension that they were actually dead. I thought of these spirits as the most pathetic ones unable to even realize that by repeating the same mistake over and over they would accomplish absolutely nothing more than to torture themselves.

"You are dead, go to the light and leave me be," I said, starting to get irritated as the rain was pouring down in a steady stream and I could see the glowing windows of the Waterside Brewery just up the corner beckoning to me like a lighthouse beam.

"Do you think you can get away from us? I have a paper that says that you are mine and I can do with you what I want," the vocal ghost began to recite what he had probably been saying for the past hundred years.

"Listen, I would love to stay and chat but it is wet and cold and I have had a really crap couple of days," I started to say when I saw two new figures moving down the street behind the two ghosts. As the vocal ghost kept on with his tiresome diatribe I suddenly could make out the shapes of two Stetson hats and the realization that "the Strangers" were gliding toward us froze me to the bone. I felt glued to the pavement as "the Strangers" were essentially sneaking up on the two ghosts or coming straight for me, of which I wasn't sure. Then like a surge my flight instinct went into high gear and I bolted across the street and hit a dead run not looking back even when I heard the two ghosts howling like wounded animals. I could see the light of the bar just ahead and I almost tripped on the wet pavement as the increasingly terrifying high pitched sounds of what I could only imagine was the devouring of two souls by "the Strangers" continued to ring in my ears. As I reached out to open the bar door the street went silent again except for the sound of the pouring rain. As I slipped inside I quickly glanced out at the now empty street. The ghosts and "the Strangers" had vanished.

I must have looked a fright. When I turned back into the bar it became evident that I had caught everyone's attention. There wasn't a single patron that wasn't staring at me. There was a table over in the corner with my least favorite group of football players from high school who were now all working either in the lumber mill or the paper mill. The burliest of the group was named Josh and he was easily the least intelligent of the bunch so when he piped up to say "Hey Charlotte, it looks like you've seen a ghost," and the rest of the table broke out into laughter I wasn't entirely surprised. But I think they were surprised by the scowl that I shot back at them or at least enough so that their jeers were cut short. It was always a struggle for the Winships to control what Margot called "zingers" or in other words letting a hex slip out in anger or frustration. And having my nerves on edge certainly didn't help so I was thankful to see Gavin step out of the back room and come straight to me with a smile on his face and a bit of a scornful look at our former classmates.

It seemed like Gavin had grown overnight and while he had always been tall it was as if the rest of his body had finally caught up with him and filled out his chest and arms to do away with any leftover teenage awkwardness. He wrapped his arm around me and led me to what I had a feeling would become our new "usual" table. When one of the waiters passed by he ordered two of something he called "strange brew."

"Not that I want to agree with those idiots but you are looking a little pale Charlotte, are you ok?" Gavin asked as we settled into the chairs. I was very glad to be facing the front door so I could keep an eye on who came in, not that I would know what to do if "the Strangers" came bursting through the doors anyway.

"I've been seeing some really strange things these days, Gavin, and you know that is saying something coming from me. I'm just not sure where it is all leading," I said and went on to tell him about everything that had happened. It was like getting a huge weight off my chest since I knew that if anyone could keep a secret it was Gavin. Ever since we had been kids we had shared all our fears and secrets. No matter how strange my vision of the world was Gavin never once faltered in being a completely devoted friend. He knew I wasn't delusional and also knew about how powerful the Winships were so I drank down his strange brew and told him everything right down to the terrifying devouring of the ghosts that I had just witnessed before crashing into his bar. There was also another reason why I needed to tell Gavin what was happening and that was that he was one of the smartest people I knew. If there were dots to connect that I was too close to see, he would recognize them or at least confirm my suspicions. So as I sat telling him the details and showing him parts of Father O'Malley's journal I could see the cogs and wheels turning rapidly as he took all the information in.

In true Gavin form he went to his office and came back to the table with a big yellow legal pad and a pen and began making a small chart with all the events from past to present with little notes in-between. As I looked over his chart and helped him fill in the blanks I could only see a series of coincidences. The most glaring connection was the strange name "Malek" that Morgan had shouted and the letter of the entity that possessed Father O'Malley as being an "M." The connection of fire was obvious but I still didn't know what "the Strangers" where or what they wanted from us. And worst of all what had burned Morgan and whether or not he would ever recover or if we were indeed going to be having a funeral on Friday as Deidre's intuition had suggested. As I watched Gavin list and connect the lines to the names on his paper my mind, instead of becoming clearer, became more and more clouded. It was like reaching into the surf to grab a shell and just when your hand would almost be on it a wave would roll in and sweep it back into the sand. I couldn't focus and I wasn't sure if it was just fatigue or Gavin's brew or a bit of both so I just sat back and observed the room for a moment.

As I scanned around the large bar I saw that under the dim lights, with the candles glowing on all the crowded tables, there were quite a few young women who were giving Gavin appraising looks. He had never been one to chase after girls when we were growing up. He had been so shy and also always accompanied by Kat and me but I had hoped that he would have opened up a bit in the years that I had been gone. There were several girls our age that kept walking by our table in a desperate attempt to catch his eye but he was so thoroughly engrossed in his chart that it was almost humorous to watch his complete obliviousness to their strutting. I made a mental note to point this out to him on another day when things in my life weren't so dire but for now I just enjoyed the spectacle.

"Well, I see a lot of connections with fire, dates and of course the fact that the name Morgan shouted also starts with an 'M' like Father O'Malley's entity but I honestly don't know what any of it means. And these 'Strangers' are a complete mystery to me although I can tell you right now that they scare the shit out of me," said Gavin as he lifted his head from the completely covered sheet of paper. "Sorry Charlotte, I know that isn't much help but let me mull it all over and in the meantime if you need me day or night please call. I do not like the idea of 'the Strangers' lurking outside of your house or Annie's house for that matter."

"I will," I said, feeling suddenly exhausted, "I have to get home Gavin, I need to rest a bit before I take over at the hospital later tonight." He gave me a worried look and refused to let me walk back to my car alone. As we made our way down the street toward Mr. Gunn's café I felt a sudden rush of nostalgia at walking down the street with Gavin like old times. Being away three years had felt like an eternity when I was going about my daily life in Seattle working in my studio, coming home at night to be with James and doing all the mundane activities in-between. But here it all felt so familiar and comfortable despite the "Graves" reputation that stuck to me. Or the extremely condensed population of spirits that always seemed to want my attention in this town. We got into the car and I drove him back to the bar using the excuse of the pouring rain as a reason for me to give him a ride although I knew that both of us were thinking about "the Strangers" lurking in some dark doorway.

"I'm going to look this over tonight and let me know if you find anything else in the journal. But please be careful, Charlotte, I don't know what I would do if I lost you," he said with an intensity that I had rarely seen in him. Before I knew it he had shut the door and was back in the bar. All I could think of was that the loss of his Great Aunt only a few years before must have made him feel the dangers of death more closely than those who are free of the burden of having lost a loved one. I sat there for a moment watching the rain wash down the windshield in a torrent and finally made my way back up the hill to Willow Street where surely Margot was waiting for me.

CHAPTER 17

As I stepped into the house I could hear Margot on the phone with Bee telling her about Morgan's condition. I quickly popped my head into the kitchen to give her a quick hello and made my way upstairs to my room in the turret. It was storming harder now and the lights would occasionally blink on and off with each large gust of wind. The grandfather clock was ticking away in the hallway of the second floor and I noticed that it read 8 p.m. as I walked by it and continued to trudge up to the third floor. I would be able to get an hour or two of sleep before heading back to the hospital to take over for Deidre at midnight.

Finally in my room, I quickly switched out the first of the monk's journal for the second one from under the mattress and used the same borrowed book sleeve to cover its exterior before putting it back in my bag. I set my alarm and sprawled out on my bed without turning off the light. I could still hear the screams of the downtown ghosts' encounter with "the Strangers" and it just felt irrationally safe to leave the light on.

As I closed my eyes I thought about the second mysterious fire that had happened in Morgan's youth. It had been around the time when he and Deidre turned 18. It was their senior year at Port Townsend High School -- a huge brick edifice that sat high above the west side of town and looked straight across the valley over to the Eisenbeis Monastery. It was an austere building that looked more like a 19th century English workhouse that one read about in books by Dickens than a nurturing learning institution. I too had attended this school although the east wing was closed off as the fire damage that had raged through it had been too severe to be repaired in the twenty five odd years that separated my attendance and my uncle's.

All that I knew of the incident had been gathered through town rumors and the occasional eavesdropping that I had done in my childhood as the grown-ups had been chatting away in the kitchen, when I was presumed asleep. Morgan had been the object of town ridicule from early on although it was more of a spiteful backhanded abuse than an obvious bullying. Deidre had eventually made friends and was by far the most integrated into the town of the Winships with her sunny personality and rather chatty spirit. Morgan had remained dark and brooding. One thing that had also set him apart from the other students was his apparent brilliance at all things mathematical and musical. He had an ease with numbers that made his instructors both awestruck as well as uncomfortable in the thought that he would surely surpass them all.

He spent most of his afternoons in the school music room where he would compose his own music on the old, and somewhat out of tune, pianos that were made available to students. Lost in his world of melodically arranged notes and phrases he would often lose track of time and would linger at the school until well after dark.

The rumors that I had heard throughout my life had something to do with a curmudgeonly teacher named Mr. Horigan who had done everything to make Morgan's high school life miserable. It was said that the frustrated old teacher had taken an instant disliking to Morgan from his first year there and seemed bent on preventing him from having an academic future. Apparently Morgan simply ignored the man by looking straight through him in class with a coolness that I believed to be one of his more chilling demeanors. The result was that Mr. Horigan had sabotaged all chances of Morgan getting in to a music conservatory despite the many operas that he had submitted across the country.

It had all come to a head one evening when Morgan was constructing a series of musical pieces in the piano room. Mr. Horigan had come in to taunt Morgan with yet another early entrance refusal that he had surely arranged. No one knows what took place as Mr. Horigan was struck mute on that night and refused to convey any information to anyone until his death many years later. But that night the east wing of the school had gone up into sudden flames and even when experts where brought in to examine the building there were no discernible sources of the fire's origin. Morgan and Mr. Horigan had been the only two people in the building that night. All that was known was that Morgan walked out of the main entrance unscathed while the building burnt itself down to the brick. Mr. Horigan became a reclusive mute for the remainder of his life.

Later that year Morgan was accepted to a prestigious university in Seattle with a full scholarship for him to study mathematics. Sadly from that night on he had never to my knowledge touched a piano again. As I slowly drifted to sleep I tried in my conscious mind to put together all the fiery parallels between Morgan and Father O'Malley. I could picture him looking out from the burnt north tower of the monastery across to the west tower of the high school.

Soon I began to dream and I could see the last image I had of Morgan running out of his house as it burnt to the ground and left only the old cider mill standing. The dream then switched to an image of Father O'Malley standing at the water's edge naked and staring out into the black water with a purplish pink sky overhead. Tears were pouring down his face as he looked to the sky and put his first foot into the wild water with its November currents. Soon he was up to his waist. His skin was a bluish grey and his teeth began to chatter uncontrollably as he continued to sink deeper into the seaweed that swirled around him, choking and tangling in his legs. Then he was pulled under, his body like a large white fish dragged into the deep with eyes rolling and arms outspread like Christ on his cross. He was gone into the currents and lost forever.

I shuddered awake as the alarm began to sound in the quiet room. As I rolled over and switched it off I could almost feel the cold waters wrapped around me like they had Father O'Malley. I took a quick steaming hot shower in the hopes that it would warm me up before I headed out into the damp night but I couldn't shake the image of Father O'Malley knowingly walking to his watery death. As I quickly got dressed and quietly made my way through the silent house I said a quick prayer for Margot to be safe here alone and made my way up to the hospital.

If I had thought that hospitals were bad during the day, they were all that much worse at night. I parked my car in the visitors' lot and rushed back through the familiar sliding doors and down the now eerily silent hallways. The sounds of breathing machines pumping air in the lungs of the dying echoed in my ears along with the occasional moan of pain or loneliness that escaped a patient's lips. As I rounded the corner to Morgan's room I spotted Deidre sitting in the folding chair by the observation window patiently reading a magazine.

"My turn," I whispered, as I leaned in and gave her a hug.

"I think I need to sleep for a week but a few hours might be just enough," she said with a weary smile. "I've been painting death scenes filled with crows for months and I guess I now know why."

My mind couldn't help but flash to the dead crow from earlier in the day but I kept it to myself. The overhead florescent light a little bit farther down the hall was blinking in a random series of flickers and I could almost feel the amusement that this offered the increasingly present demons that scurried from room to room.

"Go get some rest and I know Margot will be here at 6am. Did anything unusual happen while I was gone?" I said, thinking immediately of my encounter with "the Strangers" and she assured me that everything had been quiet here. I told her about the devouring of the two ghosts downtown. She shuddered when I described their screams and I could see that she was feeling the same panic that had filled me.

"I'll call if anything happens and be careful going home, ok?" I said. And with that she made her way to the exit as I settled in for a six hour watch over Morgan. Looking into the observation room I could see that nothing had changed and that he was still facing the ceiling. His mysterious burns were as they had been this morning. Under my breath I whispered the word "Malek" but he didn't move. The hospital had a grim stillness about it. I almost preferred the bustle of visitors, doctors and nurses to this artificial calm. I settled into the chair and while I knew that I could probably read the monk's journals in peace I almost felt like being this close to Morgan and reading Father O'Malley's words could be dangerous. Their connection was not yet clear but it was a close one and I could feel the darkness around Morgan in a visceral way.

So instead I began to think about "the Strangers" and what it was that they could want. Obviously sucking souls was part of their routine but to what end I had no clue. I had never felt anything like them before with the overwhelming power that emanated from them and the otherworldly demeanor that they held. I could hear the wind picking up outside as I tried to think back to stories that I had heard about anything similar but my mind kept drawing a blank. The flickering light at the end of the hall was becoming more agitated as the night wore on. As I pondered, I would periodically glance at it as I sat alone in the hall. Then as a large gust of wind hit the building the lights all flickered off. When they came back on again with a bright flash I saw "the Strangers" standing under the now vibrant light only ten feet away. They were staring at me unmoving and I could feel a rising scream catch in my throat as they began inching towards me. As the light continued to flicker on and off they appeared closer with each black out. The scream finally escaped my lips and before I could fully understand what was happening I realized that Samir was shaking me awake. I had fallen asleep and had nearly woken the entire hospital with my nightmare scream. It took me a few minutes of nervous glances at the still flickering light and the empty hall to put it all together.

"I'm so sorry, I was having a horrible dream," I said to Samir as he looked at me with dark worried eyes that revealed both a doctor's and a father's concern. I assured him that I was fine and that I would just read for a while until Margot came. When I asked him what time it was he said it was 3 a.m. on the dot. For the next three hours my eyes were wide open with a paranoid scanning of the halls. Nothing stirred and soon morning arrived, and with it Margot.

CHAPTER 18

When I opened the door at the Winship house after the long night's watch over Morgan I could feel the hush of the rooms welcome me in to rest. There is something very unique about having a home that has been in a family since the day it was built. It withstood the chaos of generations of births, deaths and all the life in-between. In a way it becomes another member of the family with its quirky faults and wrinkles that grow dearer over time to the people within its walls. Today in-particular, it was a blessing to have a safe place to rest before the certain arrival of the tempest.

As I headed down the hall towards the kitchen, with the intention of making myself a deliciously simple piece of toast with Bee's apple butter, the phone began to ring with its usual urgency. I was quick to pick it up thinking it was Deidre or Margot but was surprised to hear James speaking on the other line.

"Charlotte?" I could hear the strain in his voice. I knew that he had probably had many a restless night since I had made my way here on Monday. I realized that it was already Wednesday morning and I had barely spoken to him in the past two days. And while I still felt that it was not the right moment in time to let him in on all there was to know about the Winships, I felt a longing to hear his voice assuring me that all would be well.

"I just got home from the hospital, I was watching over Morgan through the night in case…" I had to pause to think of the right words since I couldn't very well tell him about "the Strangers" or the hospital demons or anything else of that nature. "He has taken a turn for the worse. We are taking shifts."

"How is he? Do they know any more about how he could have been burnt so badly? Do the doctors think he will pull through?" asked James with such genuine concern that it made my heart hurt. I reached over and managed to pull a chair closer to the phone and got comfortable for what I was sure would be a long talk.

"The doctors have no idea really so we are just waiting to see." I explained the burns and the mysterious way in which he turned up. James began to try to find logical explanations for all the events. He was an architect by trade and I could imagine him at his drafting table in our living room scribbling as we talked trying to make sense of things. He saw the world like one of his buildings, there was a foundation and all that was built on top of it had a purpose and solid reason for existing in the space whether it was functional or aesthetic. But all the things that I knew existed outside of the tangible fabric were completely alien to James. While I knew that one day in the very near future I would have to tell him about my vision of the world, today was not going to be that day. So I listened and imagined that life really was as simple as Morgan falling onto an oddly shaped element that burned his skin in the corresponding pattern. And that someone simply dropped him off when no one was looking as he or she was fearful of being inculpated in a death. If only it could be this straightforward my heart would still be desperately sad in the resulting torment of Morgan but at least I wouldn't have two fiendish "Strangers" lurking around and a ghostly monk who needed me to read his memoirs.

"James, tell me about what has been happening at home, I just need to hear about something else for a while," I asked, suddenly feeling weary.

"My project is coming along well and I have two more consults tomorrow morning," he said, "The house feels ridiculous without you in it. I forgot to change the coffee pot setting yesterday and it went off at 6am for you instead of 7am for me and when I woke up I wondered why you hadn't already had a cup until I remembered that you weren't here." I could hear the smile on his face as he spoke. "Four of your shops called and want to get orders in for Christmas. I saved the messages but figured you would call them back later." He went on with the daily things that we usually went over in the evenings. His family, our friends, work and all the small things that make up a life. I could feel my throat tightening as he went on and I realized how little we had been apart in the two years since we had been a couple. And yet I had this whole other part of me that he knew nothing about.

"Charlotte, I am coming to Port Townsend after work on Friday. I don't care what you say, it is time that I saw your home and I want to be there for you," he said with a firmness that hinted at some prior practice of the words.

"It's just that, there are some things that you don't really know about this place and my family and things are definitely a mess right now," I said, feeling the weakness of my excuses and the deep longing that I felt for him to be at my side regardless.

"I'm coming. I will be on the 7 p.m. ferry and should get there by 10 or 11 depending on the weather. How is the storm there?" he asked and I realized that the wind was again picking up after a very blusterous night.

"The power has been flickering on and off most of the night and I have a feeling we might lose it today if the wind takes down any trees," I said as I glanced out the window and could see the willow swaying in the wind and a few of the large pine trees bending with the gusts. One of the hazards of living in the "Emerald City" and its environs was the abundance of very large evergreen trees that were always placed precariously close to power lines. It was inevitability that much of the peninsula lost power for stretches at a time in winter. Even Seattle had its share of downed trees and power lines to contend with each year.

Finally I agreed to his coming and gave him the Winship address and some directions on how to get to town. I told him that if I wasn't there he could come to the Waterside Brewery, since he knew Kat and Gavin already from their visits to Seattle, or straight to the hospital. I had the strangest feeling of panic at having to finally tell him about the family "gifts" and also the most amazing sense of relief. I knew that I had put things off for too long. I was living in the bliss of a normal life but it was time now for James to know all there was to know about me. Either he would accept my "Graves" past and present or he would walk away.

After hanging up the lights began to blink again and then with a loud click all the lights on the block suddenly went out. It was still dusk outside with the morning light creeping in through heavy cloud cover so I lit one of the half melted votive candles that sat in front of

Margot's shrine. It would give me enough light to get upstairs where I could then light the turret room candles. Even though I should have been exhausted and ready to fall into a deep morning sleep, I felt a nagging that I knew would keep me awake. It was time to read the second of Father O'Malley's journals.

Chapter 19

My turret room reached up into a perfect point and was easily the highest point of the house. It was also one of the highest points in town since the Winship house was on the cliffs overlooking downtown and the bay. Being that high up meant that the wind rattled the windows and whipped around the cone hat of a roof with such speed that you could almost hear the wind talking. Today it sounded more like a steady scream as the wind grew louder and the crashing waves on the downtown shore could be heard in unison with the gusts.

Under the warmth of blankets with the candles lit on my bedside table I slowly opened Father O'Malley's second journal. I immediately noticed that his penmanship was not the original lovely curls and loops of a practiced hand as in his first journal but was now a rather hurried and harsh script. I shuddered as I started to read, both from the cold in the room as well as the words that I knew would again begin to haunt me.

September 2nd, 1953
The autumn has begun here and with it I feel a cold in my bones that is unlike anything I have ever experienced. Everything is beginning to shift into shades of fiery red and urgent yellow with a crisp morning air that makes me feel damp from the inside out. It is a strange thing to have the dying of the year come along as Father Benedict has finally broken through and can begin to remove the entity. It gave us its name yesterday after tortuous weeks spent with it battling within my skull and my body until finally my voice took on a deep intonation and the word "Malphus" rang from my lips. Father Benedict was stunned when the name spilled forth and while he tried to hide his fear there was a moment when it was written clearly across his shocked face. He is sure that it is a demon that is placed in the upper levels of the hierarchy of malevolence which will make it all that much harder to remove. But now that I know its name I feel a power that I haven't felt since this began all those years ago in San Francisco when the darkness began to creep in. If it has a name

then it is real and not just my sick imaginings or Father Benedict's invention or a mutual illusion created by our own beliefs in good and evil. This name is completely foreign to me and to have it spring forth from my lips with such certainty gave me the sense that this is not all in vain.

September 5th, 1953
I have not left the monastery since the utterance of the entities' name and while I have been praying with constancy and devotion, the likes of which has even come to the attention of the other priests, it is not without trouble that I divert my thoughts from Margot Winship. Father Benedict has come to tell me that Malphus is a demon who is known to direct 23 other demons and he is often called the crow. I am not sure what all of this means except that the more information we can gather about this entity the more we can use it to fight it out of my withering body. I seem to be losing weight at a rapidity that frightens even me but the thought of nourishment often leaves me sickened and I am unable to ingest even the most banal of foods. My other primary reason for nausea is that I can smell Margot Winship every time I step out into the monastery gardens. The roses are still blooming through the cold change of the season and the bewitching perfume makes my loins tighten with thoughts of her that then leave me feeling guilty and ill with a lust that can only be a product of Malphus' design. That I can be rid of this evil spirit and return to a monastic life free of these absurdly carnal longings that divert my piety and leave me frustrated with thoughts of unspeakable violence. Tomorrow Father Benedict will begin the first step towards the separation of me and the entity.

September 9th, 1953
I have been in the infirmary of the monastery for two days now after the first attempt at removal through invocation of the entity. It seems that Father Benedict took it upon himself to call upon Elsiba Winship for more information about the ways in which she would go about removing this creature from within me. I can only assume that consulting with an agent of the devil seemed like a good idea to him at the time but it has left me burnt from the inside out along my arms and the upper half of my torso. The burns are like nothing that anyone here has ever witnessed as they make up a pattern almost like scales although not on the exterior of the skin but rather bubbling up from beneath. It seems that Elsiba instructed Father Benedict to "fight fire with fire" as she put it and that in order to scourge the entity from me he was

to call on the four elements and the beings of light to remove this demon. While it is rumored around town that Margot has a natural gift to control water and cause storms it seems that Elsiba is known for calling on spirits to do her bidding. One priest told me that he overheard her one day in town whisper under her breath the name "Hecate" and then something to the effect of "do my will" and a split second later a car crashed into a nearby tree and killed the occupants inside. To think that Father Benedict associates with these women and seems at home with them makes me wonder about where his true devotion lies. Either he is too kind hearted and imagines himself as doing Christ's will in trying to convert what he may see as our very own "Mary Magdalene's" or he is in league with them. All that I know is that the burns are scorching me from the inside out and I can feel the demon inside me writhing and wrapping itself around my organs, burrowing into my soul.

I re-read this entry several times and then stopped to let the words sink in. It could not be a mere coincidence that Father O'Malley's burns sounded remarkably similar to Morgan's but on a less extreme level of severity. I had always known that the thing that hovered around Morgan like an ominous storm cloud was something demonic. There was a difference however in the way that the entity lurked around him. It was as if Morgan could control it in a way that I was sure Father O'Malley could not. Could this be the same entity that hopped from one to the other? What had been the catalyst to release the one and open the other to its presence? I knew that these things existed although my immediate knowledge was far more linked to the likes of the human dead and not the demonic, so it was a mystery to me although I was now positive there was a connection. I continued to read the monk's words in the hopes that they would shed more light on what this demon was and how the two were interconnected.

September 10th, 1953
The pain has eased up slightly and the marks that these strange burns left have begun to fade back under the skin. The scales that swirled up my arms have gone from black to a purplish red overnight and I can hear the entity whispering in my ear constantly. It claims that for me to be free of it I must kill the witch or give it a new host that will be of more value to it than

me. It cackles and lists names I have never heard of in random successions and with a rapidity that makes my weakened head spin. I have left the infirmary and gone back to my room for prayer and seclusion as I fear that the entity will whisper the name of a fellow priest and I will be in such a helpless state of misery that I will harm one of my brothers. The Winship women certainly are distasteful to this creature and it talks of all the insidious ways that they have slithered into the hearts and lives of the town. Their repulsive breeding with the men while feeding the innocent women with superstitions and greedily living off the treasures that were long ago stolen from the tombs of ancients by the Winship men before them. Again it tells me that killing the witch will set me free but I know that it would never be that simple and that as much as I would love to eliminate the source of my desire and obsession I fear that it would only condemn me further. Elsiba has been to visit Father Benedict and brought him some of her cursed charms and instructions for removing the creature or as she says "binding it and sending it back to hell." The temptation to believe in her is great but then the darkness has been getting harder and harder to keep at bay. I do not know what will become of me but I fear the worst as either this beast will burn and blister my body from the inside out slowly but surely or I will eventually take my own life and possibly others as well.

September 11ᵗʰ, 1953

Father Benedict tried again to remove Malphus this time with the aid of Elsiba's charms but it has left me again broken in body and spirit. I have begun to have intense migraines in addition to the new burns that cover my legs and arms alike and while before the torturous inflictions were limited to my body alone this time Father Benedict suffered an attack as well. I have no memory of lunging at him but do so I did and with a vehemence that took him completely off of his guard. Moments later I awoke on the floor with him staring down at me while holding his neck, blood streaming through his fingers from the terrible gash. Upon later examination it looked for all the life of me like a snake bite with his veins weaving a violent purple color around the wound. Being originally from the California desert if I hadn't known better I would have sworn that a rattlesnake had struck at him and left its venom coursing towards his heart. He tried to assure me that this type of attack was normal in the removal and that we must be patient and not give up hope. This parasitic evil that has latched on to me has become unsettlingly quiet since the attack and I wonder when it will rear its ugly head again and who will be its next victim.

I continued to read through the morning and as the days stretched into September the exhaustive effort of Father Benedict seemed to give Father O'Malley only brief moments of tranquility. The entity did not want to let him go. Margot's name became a rant of his as Father O'Malley's plans to kill her began to slowly form on the page as his hope lessened with the passing days.

Even though I obviously knew that Margot was alive and well it still frightened me to think that completely unbeknownst to her this tortured man had been planning her demise. I imagined her pruning her roses and humming in her garden as George came home from work each day with his usual good humor and gentle spirit. She was almost to the end of her pregnancy. Margot had probably set up the dusty pram in the attic in one of the second floor rooms as the nursery. Waiting for the exciting day when she would bring home not one but two babies.

Just as I was finishing up the second journal I thought I heard a far off knock on the front door. The Winships had never bothered to install a doorbell as the old iron knocker had become a permanent fixture on the house. It was almost 10 a.m., which was a perfectly reasonable hour for someone to be knocking on the door but whoever they were they were most likely getting pummeled by the wind that was whipping around the house. I begrudgingly left the warmth of my bed, put on my jeans and one of James' old sweaters. I slid down the three flights of stairs in a darkness that only happens when everyone's power is out.

CHAPTER 20

As I pushed open the front door the first thing I noticed was the hunched over body of Gavin as he tried his best to avoid being blown off the porch. I hurried him in while glancing at the wild purple color that filled the sky and all the fast moving black clouds that sped across the horizon. Slamming the door closed quickly as Gavin slipped into the front hall I almost had a hard time pushing the lock closed as the door was rattling with the storm.

"Whahoo," yelped Gavin, "that is some wicked wind this way comes!" He shook the rain off his jacket and hung it on his usual hook on the hall coat rack. Gavin and Kat had spent an inordinate amount of time at the Winship house in our youth, to their parents' chagrin. Nothing could beat Margot's afternoon treats and George's shed out back where he made intricate paper kites for us to play with. So to Gavin this was like something of a second home. Even while I had been away in Seattle he had stopped by every week to check in on Margot especially after his Great Aunt had passed on.

"Right this way," I motioned to the kitchen "and you can help me get a fire started in the stove. I'm a city girl now, remember."

Gavin grinned and immediately got to work adding a few dry logs from the mudroom to the wood stove, crinkling up some old newspaper and then lighting one of Margot's extra-long matches to get the fire started in several places. In a few minutes the logs were ablaze and the fire going strong. I already had the kettle on top to get some hot tea in the soaking wet man that stood before me.

"So how can I help you, sir?" I asked, enjoying our little banter before heading into the more serious topics of the matters at hand.

"Last night after you left the bar I kept thinking about everything you told me and I had planned to look up Malek. But when I got home the power was already out down by the lagoon." He settled into Margot's chair and I moved into my usual spot closest to the fire. "Anyway, 'the Strangers' had been in the back of my mind all night as I worked in the bar and I couldn't help but overhear some of the locals talking."

When you live in a town as small as Port Townsend, with its six-thousand living residents not to mention the souls that lingered, news of strange things happening travels fast especially in the one and only bar. The liquor tends to loosen otherwise careful tongues and soon there is a buzz of information moving in little waves through town. I could only imagine that the news of Morgan and his strange burns was a main topic of conversation and I wondered what the locals thought of the odd accident that had left him comatose.

"They're talking about Morgan, aren't they?" I said, feeling slightly resentful that the man they all went to with their fears and longings was also the source of so much anxiety for the church-going town folk.

"Well, that's the thing, Charlotte," said Gavin. "They aren't really talking about him anymore. They are talking about two tall and pale men that all the children in town keep seeing but no adults have been able to witness."

The words hit me with the sinking sensation that I could only equate with receiving grave news. The kettle began to chirp and as I poured us the two cups of Margot's herb tea I couldn't help but feel a deep dread at what these "Strangers" were up to in my town.

"What are they seeing?" I asked, hoping Gavin had eavesdropped enough on the customers to give me a good idea of what was happening.

"The two men were spotted in the Zellerback house in the twins' playroom. It just about scared their mother to death when the girls started giggling and screeching. When Carol went in to check on the ruckus the girls just pointed to the corner and described the two men but she couldn't see a thing. Also Robert Castle's boy started talking about them yesterday and refused to leave his room until he had drawn about twenty pictures of the two men standing side by side with old fashioned hats on. And the Mason kids all claimed to have played with two men in the back yard until one of the boys threw a rock at a crow and killed it with the stone. They all swear that one of the two men brought the crow back to life and then disappeared into the mist."

"I'm usually used to this kind of thing, but Gavin, this is getting really bizarre," I said, remembering the sounds of the ghosts being devoured the night before and the dream of "the Strangers" in the hospital. I didn't know what to make of all of it so I told him instead about what I had read that morning in Father O'Malley's journal.

"So the burns sound exactly like what Morgan has all over his body," said Gavin more to himself than to me. "I guess one good thing is that the burns did start to fade on Father O'Malley. That means the burns themselves didn't kill him. I like the thought of that for Morgan."

"I am all but sure that it is the same entity that somehow jumped from Father O'Malley to Morgan before his death. But if Father Benedict and Elsiba were unable to bind it then I wonder if Morgan tried to somehow extract it on his own?" I wondered out loud as we both sipped our tea and listened to the fire crackle.

In the same way that Margot could control water, Deidre could control air and I earth; Morgan could also control fire to a certain extent and I couldn't help but think back on Elsiba's words in Father O'Malley's journal about fighting "fire with fire." Had Morgan tried to burn the entity out of him somehow with a magical cleansing and had somehow hoped to rise out of the ashes like a phoenix with the entity extracted? It seemed suddenly even more complex than it had only a few hours earlier.

"I hope you don't mind my saying this Charlotte, but you are looking a bit ragged," Gavin announced with concern. "Have you gotten any uninterrupted sleep since this all went down?"

"Well," I laughed, "gee…not really."

It so happened that as I said this Gavin was half way in to his gulp of tea and what I said must have struck him as funny because he sprayed the entire mouth full all over the table. I don't know whether it was exhaustion or just a moment when both of us needed to let off a bit of the ever building tension but we both found this hilariously funny. So funny that after almost a minute of doubled over laughing with tears pouring down our faces and the painful gulping of air, if we hadn't stopped I was sure he would have ended up with a nasty case of the hiccups.

"Oh Charlotte," he said between gasps of air as we both started to come back to ourselves "I've missed you. Kat has missed you too and we know that things are great in Seattle but I can't help but hope that you will come back here someday."

"Maybe someday," I said noncommittally. I loved this place and all my people who were in it more than I could express but it was coupled with a heaviness that weighed on me. To bear the burden of being in a town that knew every twist and quirk of your life and your families' could be exhausting. I was almost drunk with the freedom of anonymity when I first moved to Seattle. In the beginning, I would even create fake names and occupations when confronted with overly chatty people on the bus. It was exhilarating to imagine a whole new identity for myself even if only through the eyes of a stranger.

"I'm going to take off and let you get some much needed rest before you turn completely grey," he smiled, and gave me a kiss on the head as he grabbed his coat and I showed him out the front door into the wild wind outside. He promised to look up more information on "Malek" and also "Malphus" in the town library as soon as the electricity came back on. I wondered if the two could be synonyms for the same entity or if they were two separate demons. I should have gone straight to bed but decided that a quick look in the vast Winship library couldn't hurt.

Up the creaking steps I went with a new candle in the candlestick and a small bundle of wood, paper and matches to light the wood stove in the library. There was a small cast iron stove that was connected to the same flue as the kitchen stove but was a floor above in the library. A little warmth with the electric heat out wouldn't hurt if I was to spend a bit of time sorting through four walls of floor to ceiling volumes from about 150 years of ancestors collecting various works. I made my way down the second floor hall and pushed open the library door and found it to be beautifully arranged just as George had left it before he passed away. The large oak table in the center of the room was cleared of all clutter save a reading light and a writing set. All the books were neatly arranged in the built-in shelves that made up the walls of the room with the exception of two bay windows with built in window seats that looked over the bluff.

I carefully put the lit candle on the empty table and busied myself starting a fire in the small stove with my kindling bundle. When it was crackling I added one of the dry logs that were neatly placed in a basket near the stove. I could already feel the heat start to rush into the damp and cold of the room. When I turned back to the table there was a single book open next to the candle. I was sure that only a moment before when I had turned my back to light the stove the table had been empty. I did a quick scan of the room but felt only the slightest ripple of a spirit presence. Whatever had put this out for me to see had been in the room for only a second. As I slowly moved closer to see what book it was I was somewhat surprised to discover that it was a leather bound copy of William Shakespeare's Plays and Sonnets.

I had almost hoped that it had been Elsiba leaving me a book of her spells for invocation or binding or all the other things that the older Winship generations had mastered. So I was somewhat disappointed to see that it was just a book of plays even if they were some of my favorite works. Upon closer examination I found that the page was opened to Hamlet. It was the specific moment when he spies his father's ghost walking in the ramparts of his castle and speaks to Horatio before approaching the apparition. I quickly read the first page and it was only until I was halfway through the second that my eye stuck on one line in particular. The candle flame was blinking rapidly and then rose to a tall thin peak that illuminated this line perfectly:

"And therefore as a stranger give it welcome.
There are more things in heaven and earth, Horatio,
than are dreamt of in your philosophy."

It was the word "stranger" that caught my attention. I gave a quick scan of the empty room again but felt nothing. There was no other clue as to who set this out for me to read or why. Was there a lingering spirit that was telling me to welcome "the Strangers?" As much as I would have loved to have believed that their motives were innocent there was the undeniable feeling of power and fear that accompanied them in the eyes of my town ghosts. And what the ghosts feared I knew instinctively that I too should be wary of. I closed the book and began my search for a clue about "Malek" or "Malphus" in the hopes that I could find a way to set Morgan free.

CHAPTER 21

I had spent nearly two hours searching through the shelves of the Winship library and had found nothing that directly related to either "Malphus" or "Malek" although that wasn't to say that I hadn't found some intriguing reading material. There were books that dated back to the founding of the town that Cecilia Winship had written by hand. She recorded all the births with meticulous detail as she was the one-and-only midwife for miles around. In it were all the names of all the founding families. Some of them I knew to be the ghosts that had remained to keep an eye on their ancestors while haunting the Victorian houses they had built.

One of these homes was the James house which was built by Margot's great uncle Francis Wilcox James who was one of the more powerful businessmen of his time. I had heard people talk about old Francis who died in 1920 and had left many rumors in his wake. In the folded pages of the book there was a photo I happened upon, that I was sure the town's historical society would have done nearly anything to get their hands on. Margot and her mother both had often been solicited by them to hand over the vast collection of photographs and documents that had resided in the Winship house for over a century but she always refused and said it was a matter of family history.

I studied the photo of Francis and his young bride standing before the James House which is more a mansion than a simple abode. The picture had been taken in 1909 when Francis was 77 years old and his young bride was only 24 years old and a former member of the wait staff. The turrets and spires rose up behind them built with funds that were backed by a mysterious accumulation of gold that he managed to acquire in the Mohave Desert during the Gold Rush.

The scandalous second marriage was what the town always seemed to focus on. I had heard an older story around the hearth when family would gather that told of the first wife Mary Winship, who was our direct link to the James family. She had warned Francis not to build the James House in the year of 1889. She had a foreboding that it would bring them misfortune as he tried to find a way to legitimize his sudden windfall by turning it into a wood and mortar symbol of their wealth. She would wring her hands while they built the spires. Twice the east turret fell before being erected to its towering height perched on the hill above the bay. She tried to leave hidden amulets in the four corners of the foundation, as her mother had taught her, but was ridiculed by the masons. This led to even more whispers of her being a witch by the town's people. Afraid of being ostracized, Francis forced Mary to stay away from the building of the home until its completion when she would then be allowed on the premises. He was convinced that her anxiety over his masterpiece was just a whim and would pass when she saw the house and all its forms of architectural beauty. Seven weeks after moving into the James house Mary died of a strange fever. Even now people swear that in the evenings as the second tide is rolling out you can see her lantern lit silhouette standing in the window of the east turret which has remained closed off since her death.

As much as these old family stories and photos intrigued me they were getting me no closer to helping Morgan or unraveling any of the mysteries at hand so I started to stack the books to put them back in place. Just as I stood to put back the first stack I accidentally knocked over the writing set sending a shower of sharpened pencils into the air. Tired and annoyed with my clumsiness I began the process of picking them all back up again. I unceremoniously crawled on the floor under the large oak desk in the hopes of getting that last yellow pencil that had rolled under the far leg. And that was when I found the small button on the left table leg that when pushed unlocked a completely hidden compartment on the underside of the table. Carefully I opened the small trap door and put my hand inside to feel for any hidden items. When my hand fell upon a large book I could feel my heart speed up with excitement at what might be inside.

I stayed sitting on the floor under the table like a small child who had found the perfect spot to make a fort. Slowly I began to examine the book that I had extracted from the wooden structure above me. Its cover was bound in supple leather with the "uruboros" symbol of the snake swallowing its tale emblazoned on it. When I opened it to the first page my heart sank a bit as I saw the date was only from a little over three years ago. Then my heart nearly stopped as I recognized the handwriting immediately as being that of Morgan's. The pages were filled with the familiar chicken scratch that Margot and Deidre teased him about endlessly as being completely illegible. He usually responded "I do it intentionally so *you* can't read it."

The pages were filled with mathematical equations with notes written in the margins in Latin. I realized that the hurried script was all written shortly before the fire that drove Morgan from Port Townsend three years ago. Had he been experimenting with methods of removing the darkness from himself? Or was this something else altogether?

Morgan had gone off to the university to study physics although he had done so not to become a famous scientist or a respected academic but rather to learn all there was to know in order to conduct his own experiments. In his heart, Morgan had no desire for public acclaim or wealth but rather his one mistress was his constant thirst for knowledge of the unknown and how to use it in a transformational manner. In a word, he was an alchemist. His love of chemistry took him to a certain point in his experimentations but he was striving for something far more ambitious and that was complete control over the elements. There were several things that began to reappear in the book as I flipped through the pages. There were the four triangles that I recognized as being Aristotle's elemental symbols of air, earth, fire and water.

I had been given a rather vast educational experience growing up in that George had taught me all things philosophical which included Greek, Latin and French. Margot covered all things theological as well as the mystical. Deidre had encouraged my artistic side as well as teaching me the ins and outs of business. Finally Morgan spent hours showing me the subtle tricks and hidden language of mathematics. The standard education I received in grades K-12 was rudimentary in comparison and had it not been for Kat and Gavin I may have died of ennui during school hours. This was not to say that I did not read every book that I came across at alarming speeds but like Morgan my life desires lay elsewhere than the traditional path that most followed.

So as I scanned through the pages I also noticed that inside each of the triangular symbols there was also a corresponding letter that I was quick to deduce stood for the first letter in our names. The upright triangle with a line through the bottom had a "D" inside of it which considering it was the symbol stood for "air" made it rather obvious that the "D" stood for Deidre. The upside down triangle that stood for water had an "M" in it which I assumed was Margot. The upside down triangle with a line across the base that stood for earth had a "C" in it which I knew stood for my name and lastly the right side up triangle which was fire had another "M" in it which I assumed stood for Morgan. All of these symbols were spread through the pages in semi code form and within it all the symbols for earth and the butterfly diamond appeared throughout.

It seemed that he was indeed trying to find a catalyst of some sort that would help him achieve both a physical and a spiritual evolution. There were a series of pages where he hypothesized how to remove what he had named "the impurity" or "impuritas," as he referenced it, in order to achieve a new level of control over the elements. As soon as I read the words impurity I knew that he was talking about the entity that was always hovering and the hold that it had on him. In his last hurried entry he wrote that he needed to find the source of the catalyst in order to proceed with the ceremonial fire. It seems that as he was the one who needed transformation it would be impossible to use himself as the element of fire which is a traditional catalyst for initiating a process as well as completing one. Then on the last page he wrote the key is "Mal'ak." I felt a chill run through me as I could hear the word spoken on his lips in the hospital as he lay in a coma. What I had heard as "Malek" was really written "Mal'ak" and while it looked like something that could be as old as Aramaic I could not seem to conjure its meaning from my memory. I had the feeling if I just concentrated hard enough my groggy and sleep deprived synapses would start firing and make the connection for me. Just as I started to feel the beginnings of an epiphany I heard the front door creak open downstairs.

The wind seemed to have died down a bit although the power was still off. I could hear Margot's familiar steps in the hallway on the first floor. It was already 3 p.m. and Deidre must have taken over her watch of Morgan at the hospital so Margot could come home and rest. I quickly slid Morgan's book back inside the hidden compartment in the desk and closed the trap door until it clicked shut while grabbing the yellow pencil that had brought me under the table to begin with. I tidied up the table by quickly returning the stack of books to the shelf and made my way downstairs to see if all was well. My mind was still swirling with the myriad of symbols and meanings that were so diligently recorded in Morgan's own hand.

CHAPTER 22

As I made my way down the steps I could hear the familiar sounds of Margot in her kitchen lighting the wood stove. It was followed by the sound of water filling the kettle finished with a snap of the lid so it would boil quickly. The scrape of the legs of her wooden chair on the uneven floor made a squeak and the wood cracked as she settled into her usual spot. I could smell the perfume of roses all the way down the hallway. When I reached the kitchen she looked up and smiled at me over her reading glasses. She had a small notebook in her hands and she quickly set it aside and told me to pull up a chair.

"Has anything changed since this morning?" I asked and she slowly shook her head to indicate that it hadn't, almost as if speaking the words was too much for her.

"I was going to go over to Annie Christy's to bring her some extra candles for the storm but I am just so tired I could hardly make it back home," Margot said, and I could see her eyelids nearly half closed as she waited for her tea.

"I'll take them over right now," I offered, feeling like it was the least I could do. I had been having a nagging feeling about Annie being alone since she told me about "the Strangers" making an appearance at her back door. It would ease my mind to check in on her.

Margot had a little basket of things for me to take over including candles, a flashlight with new batteries, several golden delicious apples from Deidre's apple tree and a tin filled with herbs for tea. I put on my shoes not looking forward to going out in the storm but at least feeling useful in the immediate. I gave Margot a quick hug and made a mad dash for my car.

The wind had calmed somewhat compared to early in the morning. It had turned into just small gusts that shook the trees in intervals but the air felt electric in only the way it can before lightning and thunder are about the strike. The sky was a shocking purple with ripples of blue and magenta. It had been years since I had seen such a combination of colors splashed through the clouds. As I made my way out to North Beach I ran the symbols from Morgan's notebook through my mind. It came to me that the M in the fire symbol most likely stood for "Mal'ak" and not Morgan as he could not be the catalyst for fire alone, but who was this creature? Was it as much responsible for Morgan's condition as Malphus was for Father O'Malley? Had he gone looking for it after the fire that destroyed his home?

When the third fire had occurred three years ago, Morgan had been acting strange for months leading up to the blaze. He had become even more withdrawn than usual and even Deidre was having a hard time getting him to leave the cider mill for a few hours. He had cloistered himself inside with books piled high. He had even abandoned the usual apple harvest that year leaving all the fruit to rot on the branches of his small orchard. Margot had been acting odd as well and while Deidre and I had repeatedly mentioned how worried we were about Morgan's extreme solitude she refused to say anything to him.

The last time I saw him Deidre and I had just pulled into the driveway. His cabin was engulfed in flames. The timbers were groaning as the roof began to collapse in on the structure. Deidre ran screaming to the nearest neighbor to get the fire trucks out immediately. That was when I saw a movement in one of the front windows. I had been frozen in place unable to react to what appeared to be Morgan trying to make an escape from the inferno that had swallowed all that he owned in the world. The breaking of glass as a chair came flying out the front window was what finally dislodged me from my shock. Before I knew it I saw Morgan climbing out of the front window, his clothes ablaze. It was almost as if fiery hands were grasping at him in an effort to contain him within the blaze. As he broke free he ran headlong into the forest with black smoke rising from his clothes. He had not given even a backward glance at us or the house in flames. It was the last time that we had seen him until just a few days ago when he reappeared comatose and burnt over ninety percent of his body with the strange swirling marks.

That day of the burning house had been a turning point in all our lives. Margot had suffered the most. Deidre has a constant nagging sensation as if a part of her was missing. And while I carried a little knot in my heart for him every time the odor of burning leaves was in the air, it had also been the moment I ventured into a new life. My family had finally given me permission to leave Port Townsend. I had to admit that there wasn't a day that had gone by since that I hadn't thought about where Morgan might be or what he was doing. I scanned crowds in the city expecting to see his familiar black hair and pale skin. On several occasions I had chased after random men on the street thinking it was him only to be disappointed by an unsuspecting innocent. Whenever I heard news of unusual fires in and around Seattle I always tried to find out as many details as possible in the hopes that an article or a news cast would mention a tall dark haired man on the scene. But nothing had ever surfaced and Margot had seemed to age more rapidly with each passing year as if wasting away with worry. She had said on many occasions that not knowing what had become of him was worse than if he had been dead. I tried to reassure her by saying that if he was dead than I would surely know but the mystery of his whereabouts had weighed heavily on us all.

Before I knew it I was past Gavin's house and making the familiar turn out to North Beach. The lagoon looked almost violet as the first flash of lightning lit up the sky. It was quickly followed by booming thunder that made my heart leap into my throat. As I turned into Annie Christy's long driveway and parked by the talisman gate I had the sudden feeling that I was not alone. I sat in the car for a moment watching the trees sway in the forest that bordered the log cabin. As I looked over to my right I noticed a man standing by Annie's Model T dressed in clothing that looked appropriate to the time period when the car was made. He was a pale grey and somber with his index finger raised to his lips instructing me to be quiet.

I turned off the engine and grabbed the basket. As I stepped out of the car the man slowly vanished. Just as I was reaching to find the latch on the gate I noticed that Annie was sitting on her porch in the rocking chair with a blanket over her legs as always. The chimes were ringing loudly as the wind was beginning to pick up again. When I finally unlatched the gate I felt the need to do as the specter had instructed and approach quietly as not to wake her with a start. As I made my way down the stone pathway amid the cacti and drift wood I noticed that her eyes were indeed closed as if in sleep. Her chair was rocking gently like the wind moving one of its trees. When I finally set foot on the covered landing I spoke just above a whisper:

"Annie, it's me, Charlotte."

Her eyes were still closed and as I got closer to her I could feel a tightening in my throat as tears threatened to overflow from my eyes.

"Annie, wake up," I said with a crack in my voice as the first tear dropped from my right eye and landed on her folded hand as I leaned closer to her. There was no breath moving her tiny chest. In that moment she looked more like a young girl than a woman who liked to joke that she had seen Hailey's comet twice. I put my hand on her shoulder and gave her a light shake. Her skin was ice cold. Her mouth was curled at the corners into a little smile as if she had died while hearing a charming story or an impish joke. I knelt beside her as the sky was suddenly lit up with another lightning bolt followed by crashing thunder. It had unleashed a flurry of wind and the start of heavy raindrops.

My own tears began to crash to the ground as I hung my head and cried for Annie who had come to her end. I dropped the basket next me and an apple rolled across the porch as if in slow motion. The smell of death was still faint in the air and instead the rain gave the woods a green perfume of moss and foliage. As I cried I felt a sudden wave of fear wash over me at the thought that "the Strangers" had been here lurking at her backdoor only a day before. Had they devoured her spirit as they had the downtown ghosts? Had they taken her from us too soon and left her cold shell behind for us to find as a calling card of their passage? I felt a rising panic take hold of me as I saw the light beginning to fade. The rain had started to fall in earnest and before I knew it I was running down the path to my car. As much as I wanted to take her with me I knew that I needed to get the authorities out to the cabin and also make sure that Margot and Deidre knew what was happening.

My heart was pounding in my chest as I burst back through the talisman gate and into my car at a speed that even surprised me. My tires began to spin in the mud that had begun to accumulate in the pouring rain and after several failed attempts at getting back on the main road I finally hit pavement. I was driving at a wild pace up towards the hospital with tears drenching my cheeks and sobs rattling my body. Thankfully most of the town was tucked safely inside their homes as I skidded to a halt into the hospital parking lot and ran crying in search of Deidre.

CHAPTER 23

I was dripping water in a solid stream as I made my way down the sterile corridors. This was one of the few buildings in town that had generators strong enough to keep the electricity running even in the worst of storms. As I rounded the corner and found Deidre sitting in our usual chair by Morgan's room talking in hushed tones with Samir, I all but collapsed at her feet. In between gasps and sobs I managed to tell them that I had found Annie dead at her cabin. Before I could finish Samir had reached for a nearby phone and was already sending an ambulance over to her house. Deidre held my soaked and shaking body in her arms. She quickly joined me in crying over the loss of Annie. I whispered in her ear as best I could about my fear that "the Strangers" had taken her and what if one of us was next.

"Not now, Charlotte, we will talk about this later. For now we must take care of Annie, ok?" she said, soothing me like she had when I was just a child.

"I can't tell Margot," I said while shaking my head, "I just can't."

"I'll go now and tell her and you stay here with Morgan. If something happens don't leave the hospital. Just stay here and wait for us." Deidre let out a deep sigh. Gathering herself she gave me a kiss on the cheek as she whispered with a sound of defeat in her voice: "I guess we will be having a funeral on Friday after all."

I sat huddled in a little ball on the chair by Morgan's room wishing that I had been mistaken and that Annie had just been in a sound sleep. But I knew better than that. By now her body was probably being taken to the only funeral home in town for preparations. I could only imagine what was happening at the Winship house as Deidre was giving Margot the news of Annie's passing. Every time I closed my eyes I could see her tranquil face frozen in death. Why anything would want to harm Annie was beyond me. While it did appear that she had died peacefully I couldn't shake the feeling that "the Strangers" had been there in her last moments.

The hospital seemed quieter today than most afternoons. I slowly began to calm down as the initial shock transformed into deep sadness. I turned to examine Morgan through the glass and saw that he hadn't changed at all since this morning. He was still facing the ceiling and the darkness was still hovering all around him expanding and retracting with his every breath.

"Malphus," I said in a low whisper "is that your name?"

Nothing changed. I felt an anger rise within me as I thought back to all the damage these entities caused not just in my family but to the world at large.

"Are you the same demon that tortured Father O'Malley?" I asked in a taunting voice not expecting any answer. I could feel the darkness beginning to unfold slightly at the mention of the monk.

"So who is Mal'ak?" I said a little louder, not realizing that Samir had just turned the corner and was in earshot.

"What did you say, Charlotte?" he said as he moved towards me with his doctors coat flapping behind him like two white wings.

"Oh, nothing," I said, feeling a sudden embarrassment having been caught talking to something that most people can't see or feel.

"Did you say, 'Mal'ak'?" he said with a look of both amusement and surprise.

"Yes, I read it somewhere but I don't know what it means," I said, feeling a bit shy for my lack of knowledge in front of Samir who always seemed to know everything.

"It's an old word that people use where I am from," he said with a smile, "I think it was originally Semitic or Aramaic but it is also used today in Arabic and Hebrew. It's the name my mother calls my brother but rather sarcastically."

"What does it mean?" I asked suddenly, feeling alert and extremely interested in what Samir had to say about the mysterious name that Morgan had told me and that I had read in his notebook.

"It means 'angel'," Samir said with a sudden solemnity. "Where I was born there is always talk of many different angels, each with its purpose. They are not seen as harp playing doves but rather powerful spirits sent often to earth with a divine purpose from God.

They can be anything from a messenger to a destructive force or a guardian of the weak."

I didn't know what to say suddenly. It had never occurred to me that Morgan would call on the beings of light as my family called them. The darkness that hovered around him made me think that he would himself be drawn to the darkness. I was speechless on hearing what the word "Mal'ak" represented. Then again there were such things as dark angels.

"Charlotte, the ambulance picked up Annie and she is being examined but for all that we can see it looks like she died peacefully and naturally," Samir said as he put his hand on my shoulder in a gesture of comfort. "It was just her time and there was nothing you could have done."

"Thank you, Samir," I said, letting his words sink in slowly.

"I'll check back in a while, do you need me to bring you anything?" he said with his usual calm and collected manner.

"Maybe a cup of coffee," I said, and he nodded and continued on his rounds. For as long as I could remember Samir had always been the one to comfort Deidre and I when tragedy struck our family. He had moved to town just as my Grandfather George had taken ill. When George had passed he had helped Margot with all the funeral arrangements and had held my small child hand during the service as I trembled with cold and sadness. Losing Annie I was sure would be the same. While he had seen unspeakable tragedies both in his homeland and later in the likes of Harborview hospital he always retained his empathy for the ones left behind. He knew of my abilities to see the lingering spirits who had lost their way but unlike many he didn't find it strange at all. When I was just eleven years old he had explained to me that his mother and his sister had special gifts as well. They could see spirits that no one else could. But when it came to the intricacies of all that was happening with Morgan I felt that if anyone should tell him about it, it should be Deidre and not me.

As the hours went by and I felt the initial shock of finding Annie begin to wane into a quiet melancholy I couldn't help but think back to when George had passed away almost twelve years before. Small town life moves at a slower pace than the big cities and Port

Townsend had a special pace all of its own that moved with the tides. The early birds got up in time to comb the beaches when the low tide left sand flats for hundreds of feet out while the noon sun marked the moment when the tides would come rushing back to land. This happened again in the evening and there was a certain rhythm that moved the inhabitants of the town that could be felt according to their link to the tides. My grandfather George was a morning person and on the nights that I would stay over at the Winship house I looked forward to the familiar sounds of him rising before sun up to make his morning coffee. The lapping sounds of the nearby waters retreating from the shore were accompanied by the gurgling of the old aluminum coffee pot steeping its dark brew.

One morning as I awoke, waiting to smell the distinctive and comforting aroma of the coffee coming from the kitchen I instead found the sun blazing in through the curtains and the house strangely silent. It was then that I realized that George was sick and that the tides were getting ready to turn in his life. At first there were only subtle differences that most people wouldn't have noticed like the way his clothes hung a little loose or how he coughed more often than usual. Before I was born he had survived lung cancer which was one of the hazards of spending forty years working in the town paper mill. Morgan began to take over many of his chores and would read to him in the early evenings or play endless games of chess. As for Margot, she held her usual strong exterior but I often saw her peeking over her notebooks to wistfully look at the man who had spent forty one years by her side.

In the beginning of his illness he was still able to take Kat, Gavin and I to Fort Warden State Park to fly kites that he made in his workshop. We sat on our favorite bench and watched as his red paper dragons and crepe paper bats twisted and turned in the wind while eating peanut butter and jelly sandwiches wrapped in waxed paper. George's nickname in town was "Kite Flyer" and he could always be counted on to create a new whirligig in his little workshop under the willow tree.

As his body slowly weakened I spent afternoons by his bedside telling him all the town gossip, about the stones I had found on the beach or the ghosts that had been to visit me. Margot nursed him and he never complained about anything until he finally told her he was ready to go to the hospital. We spent the weeks leading up to Christmas at the Jefferson County Hospital bringing him a gift a day, his favorite of which was a little brown reindeer ornament that we put on the tiny Christmas tree that one of the nurses had given him. Every time we would drive up to the hospital parking lot I would try not to think of how close the graveyard was and how our place of peace and tranquility would soon be filled with my sadness.

I will never forget the night that he died as I was standing at the top of the Winship porch looking over the cliffs waiting to get in the car to rush to the hospital to say our last goodbyes. As I looked down into the complete 2 a.m. darkness of the town I could feel the eyes of every being hidden away in the frost-covered December night staring back at me. The chill ran into the very center of my bones as I looked into darkness and felt the whip of the wind and the movement of the winter tides taking with it the man who was my pillar of strength and protection. Besides Morgan, George had been the only male figure in my life after losing my father so young that there was nothing to remember of him. I was a month shy of my tenth birthday when I held George's hand as he let out his final breath. His body went completely slack and there was the distinct feel of his soul leaving the room as I held on to a rapidly cooling shell of a body that no longer held any part of the person I so loved. His face became one of a stranger and in that moment Deidre and Morgan held on to each other as Margot simply hung her head and prayed for his safe arrival on the other side.

For thirty days after his death a sparrow tapped on Deidre's living room window every morning as the tide was receding. On the one month anniversary of his death the little bird stopped coming to us. As much as I missed him I felt relieved that he was not tied to any place and was able to move on into whatever awaits us after death.

At first we all visited the graveyard together every day with the morning tide and I was greeted by the little kitten purring and brushing up against my legs. Seeing his name on the family tomb where mine would certainly be added one day in the far off future made me feel a deep longing for his presence but there was no doubt in my mind that he was truly gone. After a while we would only visit once a month and I would make a point to weed the children's graves until a new groundskeeper volunteered to take his place. This was when Samir had taken to spending more time with me as the rest of the family dealt with their grief.

As I sat sipping the coffee that Samir had dutifully brought me, in the same hospital where George had passed and Morgan was now laying helpless, I couldn't help but feel the familiar weight of grief settle in on my shoulders. It seems that Deidre's premonitions of death were right after all and now it was our time to say goodbye to Annie Christy as well. But deep down I knew that from this moment on I would fight until my last breath to figure out what had happened to Morgan and how to bring him back from this impending doom. I refused to let him be dragged into the void by an entity that had a dark fixation on my family. So as I sat there I began to run through all the strange clues that I had found since returning home. Somehow I would need to connect them all together into a weapon with which to fight "Malphus" and resurrect Morgan once and for all.

CHAPTER 24

There are many things that simply cannot be explained by modern science. One excellent example of this is the weather patterns in Port Townsend for the past 70-odd years. One minute there would be sun and the next a downpour would nearly flood the entire downtown area leaving small lakes in the middle of the street deep enough to become homes for errant frogs and fish. Tobias Gunn loved telling the story of the morning when he opened his shop and a carpe leapt from a nearby puddle only to slide across the floor into the tuna fish aisle.

The most fantastical of stories was most certainly when one hot summer night Jolene Cook began to hear the familiar plunking sound of heavy rain erupt on her tin-roofed shack that resided in the wetlands. Thinking nothing of it she went to bed and in the morning, sleepy eyed and groggy from a restless night of troubling dreams, she stepped off her front porch straight into over 20 feet of standing water. Her house was floating in the middle of what is now known as the lagoon. As she scrambled back onto the leaking floorboards half the town could hear her cursing Margot Winship as she searched for a way to pull her home to shore. So while the Seattle meteorologists scratched their heads at the seemingly schizophrenic weather patterns that had settled on Port Townsend, the town folk always turned a sour eye in Margot's direction when unusual storms hit the coast.

As I sat in the hospital I wasn't terribly surprised when I started to hear little gasps as people looked out the frosted windows at the delicate white flakes that were fluttering to the ground all over town. Thankfully the power had come back on as the winds had finally let up but the rain that had been falling was now covering the ground as a frozen blanket of snow. To say that snow in October was unusual was an understatement. And as I sat in my chair watching Morgan's comatose body I tried to ignore the sharp looks the town folk were giving me. I heard one nurse whisper loud enough for me to hear "the apples are all going to be frozen," with a harsh tone as she glanced my way. While another passerby griped "what will happen to this year's pumpkin patch" while sending me a withering stare. What they were really saying was "can't that Margot Winship control herself" but as the hours went by and news of Annie's death and coming funeral circulated through town the looks began to soften from irritation to a common mourning.

I could imagine Deidre sitting with Margot in her kitchen as she told her about my finding Annie lifeless sitting in her rocking chair on her porch. And while we all knew that Annie's life was nearing its completion it was still a shock to us all that the seemingly eternal woman had finally gone home. The snow drifted down the rest of the afternoon creating a different kind of havoc in town from earlier in the day when wind and rain where the main preoccupation. As the snow drifts slowly accumulated and the cold light began to fade on the horizon I felt the chill of loss settle over me much as I was sure it had Margot and Deidre. Samir brought me vending machine food and kept me company between his rounds until he managed to dislodge me from my plastic chair guard post by telling me that Deidre was on her way back and that she wanted me home with Margot.

As I walked into the startlingly white parking lot I noticed that it was strangely devoid of all cars except for my own which was now frozen over with a layer of fresh snow. The street lights had come back on and I could see a glow of electricity in all the homes that stretched out into the valley and up to the cliffs. The smell of burning wood was thick in the air since almost everyone had means of heating with wood in a town that had regular bouts of severe weather and downed power lines.

For a moment I had a sinking feeling in the pit of my stomach that "the Strangers" were waiting for me out in this abandoned parking lot and that I was a lamb wandering into wolves' territory. As I brushed the inch thick layer of snow off my windows I kept a keen eye out for any unexpected movements but found that everything was eerily still as I climbed inside my car with numb fingers. I inched my way back to the Winship house carefully maneuvering the slick turns and steep hills until I finally pulled in to the carriage house. I noticed that Deidre's car tracks were already beginning to disappear under a new layer of snow and the rose garden was filled with open blooms encased in the glistening white powder. As I made my way up the back steps I noticed that the kitchen lights were off and in their place was the flickering of candles. I left my wet shoes and jacket in the mudroom and as I came into the kitchen I couldn't help but be struck by the beauty of the altar that Margot had erected to honor Annie.

The Madonna statue was in her usual spot but she was now surrounded by at least thirty candles of all sizes and a black and white photo of Annie and Elsiba from the 1930s. There was a small glass of blackberry wine set out along with other small offerings including seven bouquets of Margot's roses, a nest filled with shells, the small amulet that Bee had given me on my way home and a single crow's feather.

The house was still and thinking Margot had gone to bed early in her grief I tiptoed my way up to my room, careful not to wake her. As I reached the third floor landing I froze in my tracks as I noticed that my door was ajar and inside the light was on. Had I left it on before the power went out? I was almost positive that it had been off. As I slowly pushed open the door I was shocked to see Margot sitting on the edge of my bed holding Father O'Malley's journals in her lap.

Her hands were covered with little pinpricks and a droplet of blood was hanging precariously on the tip of her index finger while she read the opened page of the first journal. There were red circles around her eyes as I was sure she had been crying since the news about Annie had reached her. She now wore an expression of both shock and hurt that I had rarely witnessed. Her usually controlled demeanor was nowhere to be seen on her grieving face. The wood floor creaked as I shifted my weight from one foot to the other and her eyes shot up to meet mine as I stood frozen in the doorway.

"I was putting new roses in your room," Margot said in a soft voice as she looked up at me and pointed to the dresser. A bouquet of her red roses was perched on it which also explained the pinpricks on her fingers. "And these were lying out on your bed." I could see the pain flash across her face not only at the horror of reading the words that Father O'Malley had written about her but also my betrayal in hiding the fact that I was reading them.

"I...," the words froze on my lips. Not knowing what to say I just looked to her and the journals trying to find an explanation.

"I never should have kept anything related to that man in this house," the hurt in her voice had suddenly turned to anger. "I should have thrown them in the ocean after him and let it all be swallowed up together into the void."

"He...," I swallowed hard building up the courage to say all that was racing through my head. "He came to me and showed me where they were." I paused, "in the attic."

Margot's silence filled the room with the same cold that was outside covering the ground with snow and ice. I could feel the lump in my throat burning as I tried to explain the events that had led up to my finding them. Including all that I had discovered about "Malphus" and how I thought it was possibly the same entity that was torturing Morgan. It all came rushing out of me in a nervous gush of words as she watched me with her cold blue eyes unmoving.

As I finished she sat silent for a moment and then stood up grabbing the journals while pushing past me into the hall.

"I know it is the same demon. Follow me," she said with a coolness that chilled me to the bone. As she made her way downstairs to the kitchen I felt like a small child after being scolded. I dutifully followed behind her and when we stepped into the kitchen that was still ablaze with both the altar as well as the wood stove's crackling flames, she motioned for me to sit. As I did she grabbed the old cast iron handle of the stove, opened it and tossed the two journals inside the flames. I couldn't help but let a small gasp escape my lips as I watched the pages curl up and catch flame slowly turning into embers.

She carefully sat herself down in her chair and fixed me with a stare that left me silent. After a few minutes of listening to the fire devour the long ago written words of Father O'Malley she finally cleared her throat and began to speak.

"I think it's time you heard my side of the story" Margot finally said as she folded her hands and sat up straight. She began to speak as the snow continued to fall covering Port Townsend in a sparkly layer of ice that people would talk about for years to come.

CHAPTER 25

It took several minutes of sitting in silence before Margot cleared her throat and began to speak. I pulled my legs up onto the chair and was careful not to move afraid that the slightest distraction would make her stop. I feared that I would never really know what had come to pass all those years ago when my Mother and Morgan were born.

"I know that you know a bit about your great grandmother Elsiba from what you have heard around town and in this house," Margot said and I nodded for her to continue. "She was a hell raiser of sorts and she made people rather nervous. Much like the way that you can receive messages from ghosts she could receive messages from all kinds of spirits both light and dark and everything in-between. As she got older she could not only receive messages but she could conjure and control these spirits in ways that were extremely complex and undoubtedly frightening.

There were many stories surrounding the accidental death of my father Louis when he had gone out fishing on a clear day and was never seen alive again. It was rumored that he had vanished at sea and that Elsiba mourned only the bare minimum after his ship washed ashore empty and without the slightest trace of incident. She had come to me that day when I was just a small girl of five and had whispered that Daddy had gone to live with the seals who loved him so much that they took him to their secret home. I knew then that my Mother had her own secrets and soon the town was alive with rumors about not only Louis' mysterious death but also Elsiba's ambiguous relationship with Annie Christy. In those days no one would say anything out loud but it was well known that they were lovers and remained so until Elsiba passed away. In many ways Annie became my second mother and taught me how to ride a bicycle, drive her old Model T and properly chop firewood for myself.

When George and I married, Elsiba moved out of the Winship

house leaving it to us to fill it with children and hopefully shift the attention of the locals from her to the new members of the family. That was when she moved in to the cider mill, which later became Morgan's home, to both be nearer to Annie and also to have the privacy and space to practice and hone the skills of her gift. During this time I began to struggle with my own gifts and their overall meaning. That is when I first met Father Benedict who you most certainly read about in those cursed journals.

He was fascinated with our family gifts and having come over from Ireland in the last part of the 19th century he was more than familiar with the hate that ignorance breeds. We spoke endlessly about each Winship woman's gift and he told me of a group of women from his village near Cork that had many similarities to our own family. But to Father Benedict these gifts were something that was given by God and meant to be used for good on earth. He refused to think of us as anything as common as the folk image of a witch. Rather he told me stories that came from the Bible about natural magic being taught to the chosen women by their angelic lovers. He was sure that we were the descendants of those very women who over the millennia had lost touch with the source of those gifts as time and man had slowly stamped out all traces of their origin.

In many ways he became the father figure I never had and also my friend, teacher and confidant. Slowly I came to hold the Catholic tradition in my heart in a truly profound way and asked to be baptized. It was the happiest time of my life and soon after I became pregnant with your mother and Morgan. It felt like it was a confirmation of my new found faith and understanding of the Winship gifts. I became increasingly devoted to the Virgin Mary and felt a deep connection to her in her humanity and her divinity. All was truly miraculous with my love for George and my happy condition. That is until Father O'Malley arrived."

Margot paused and I could see her posture go stiff just at the mention of his name. I sat waiting for her to continue enraptured by the secret life that both Elsiba and Margot had lived in their youth. All of this was unknown to me from Louis' death to Elsiba and Annie's clandestine relationship which wouldn't raise an eyebrow in my generation but in theirs was all but unheard of. No wonder the priests and the town folk talked about Elsiba in hushed tones behind her back. The fire was still crackling away beside me and I knew the two journals were now just a pile of ash but that there was still the third journal tucked away safely in my bag for the time being. Margot shifted in her chair and then continued with her story.

"I honestly had no idea about Father O'Malley's fixation with me until it was so far out of control that there was no turning back for him. I had the first inkling when George found him peeking in our living room window late one night and I am sure if he hadn't been a priest he would have lost a few teeth. I asked Father Benedict about this strange man who always seemed to be lurking around the monastery grounds scowling at me and he told me to pay him no mind. Eventually he told me that he was a troubled man who was seeking help within the order but little did I know that Father Benedict had been asking Elsiba for her help with what I would later find out was the removal of the entity.

Of course Elsiba later told me that she had felt the entity the first time she saw Father O'Malley in town and that instinctually she knew it would prompt him to come after us. She told me this was how all the witch hunts had begun and that she had sent her own protective charms into action as soon as she understood that it meant to harm me. I was the one who ensured that the Winship name continued and this entity in all its darkness wanted to not only destroy its host but also make sure that women in possession of angelic gifts were wiped from the earth entirely. And while she tried to teach Father Benedict of the ways of the spirits he could only go forth with the teachings that were appropriate and in accordance with the rules of his order.

It all came to a terrible head on November 2nd 1953 when I was eight and a half months pregnant and waiting impatiently for the arrival of your mother and Morgan. George had gone to work and I made my way to the back yard to grab the last of the chamomile that was hanging on from summer. As I slowly bent to pick the small white flowers I suddenly felt two hands wrap around my neck and squeeze with diabolical force. The next thing I remember was waking up on the floor of this very kitchen disoriented and with the sudden realization that my water had broken.

As I slowly regained consciousness I saw Father O'Malley pacing back and forth across the kitchen floor ranting to himself or rather conversing with the entity. Tears were streaked down his face. He held a kitchen knife in his left hand. He became increasingly agitated as he argued with the darkness inside of himself. It was in that moment that I let go of all that Father Benedict had taught me of turning the other cheek and trusting in God as rage began to boil over inside of me. The contractions had begun and I knew that it was time to simply be a Winship and let lose my fury on this poor soul that had dared to attack me in my own home. I carefully pulled myself up as Father O'Malley continued to pace oblivious to my standing there. At the top of my voice, I unleashed all my power in a series of words that I knew would leave this man's soul cursed for all of eternity.

He turned to me wide eyed and helpless and before I knew it he had dropped the knife and ran out the backdoor to what would be his imminent death. I had cursed him by water, my element of power, and had set in motion the wave that would drag him out to sea; lost forever. Somehow I managed to call for help and when I arrived at the hospital your mother Deidre was born only minutes after I was wheeled into the delivery room. But then the difficulties of giving birth to your uncle Morgan began. What I didn't know until later was that in the moments that your uncle was struggling to be born Father O'Malley was walking to his own watery death. In my efforts to bring your uncle into the world I was holding on to all my anger and hate at the man who had just attacked me and with that I linked the two in a terrible curse. My anger had opened a door that let the retched entity hop from Father O'Malley's now dead shell to my own child's untarnished soul.

For some reason the Winship women are immune to these types of entities which is why Deidre was left untouched but the males are vulnerable in a way that I cannot explain. My curse had come back on me tenfold in that my own innocent child now carried the burden of the darkness that had haunted the tragic priest. When it was time to take my new babies home, George was so thrilled. I kept the truth of that terrible day from him although from that moment on I lost my newfound faith. Father Benedict pleaded with me to speak with him and begged forgiveness that he had not come to me earlier to warn me of the impending danger. He and Elsiba remained friends until he passed only a few years later and it was she who had passed the sealed envelope along to me. I could not tell Father Benedict that something inside of me had snapped and that I would not forgive the evil that had destroyed my child's chance at a normal life.

As Morgan grew older, the darkness hovered and the fires began although it seemed that the fires were more of an excess of emotion much like my effect on the weather. I do not think that the fires were caused by the entity but rather they are your uncle's unique gift; however, I knew that the darkness at times enveloped him as well. He had become obsessed with the removal of the entity when he was studying at the university and eventually after he finished he came home to research in depth while making his ciders and reading cards for the town folk.

It was three years ago when he came to me with what he believed would be the way to finally extract the entity once and for all from his soul. But he needed my help. In fact, he needed all of our help and I refused him. I would not allow him to use you to break this spell." Margot paused for a moment as she fixed me with her entreating stare. I could see a pleading in her eyes for me to understand and empathize with all she had been through in secret.

"That was when he left," she said with a crack in her voice "with the fire on his heels as he set off to find another way to lift the burden that the entity had on his soul. I can only assume that he eventually tried to cast the being from himself and that is where the horrible magical burns came from. But in doing so I know that he conjured something to come to his aid in the process and that is what was following you here. I can only assume that it is 'the Strangers' and whatever he asked of them they are here to fulfill that request and also in turn reap their reward."

My mind was spinning with all the images that she had woven in her tale and also with more questions than I knew how to even begin to ask. Margot looked weak and exhausted with the effort of releasing so many secrets that she had held in more than half of her life. I slowly rose from my chair and wrapped her in my arms as she began to sob. I held my Grandmother in my arms, comforting her in this rare moment when she allowed her fragility to show through. Outside the window the snow was falling in cadence with her tears.

CHAPTER 26

Stillness settled over the house after I had helped Margot to her bedroom and tucked her in the way that she had done for me when I was a child. As I settled myself into one of the large wing backed chairs in the main parlor by the front bay windows, I watched as the snow began to fall more slowly in the lamp light. As Margot drifted to sleep the flakes became tiny frozen droplets that created a glistening cover over the lawn. The willow tree looked as if it was made of a fine white lace.

I could smell the familiar scent of cloves and wood that meant that Fox was in the room with me. He was hovering in the dark corners watching over me as I reflected on all that had transpired in just the few short days since my return home. Losing Annie at this moment in time as Morgan was at death's door was almost unbearable and yet we would have to bear it with grace and dignity as she would have wanted it.

A shrill ring sounded from the old rotary phone and when I picked it up I was relieved to hear Kat's voice on the other line.

"Oh Lottie, I am so sorry to hear about Annie," she said with genuine sadness. "Gavin and I would like to take care of the wake and have it in the bar after the service. I think Annie would have approved and I know she always told me when she finally took her leave of us she wanted a big party with no sad faces and a lot of booze." I couldn't help but smile when I heard the mention of booze. It seemed like such an old term and reminded me of Annie's quirky humor.

"I think she would have liked that a lot Kat," I said, feeling the weight of the day's events on my mind. "I will make sure that Margot and Deidre know you are organizing it. It helps so much. Thank you, Kat. And thank Gavin for us as well; I am sure I will be by tomorrow." After hanging up the phone I went back to watching the snow fall lightly on the silent town and eventually I drifted off to sleep.

I soon found myself in a waking dream where I was sitting in the same chair in the Winship parlor asleep watching myself from across the room. My body was curled up into a ball in the large overstuffed chair. As I looked over my sleeping body and out the window, I noticed fresh footprints in the snow leading up to the front porch. The front door had been left unlocked and it slowly creaked open inch by inch. A woman stepped into the hallway from the cold outside. She then came through the archway that opened into the parlor where I slept. Her long dark hair and vibrant green eyes I recognized immediately as being the woman I had seen in so many family photos. It was Elsiba Winship. As she walked into the room she grabbed a folded blanket from the couch and carefully covered me with it. Then she knelt beside the chair and began to whisper family secrets in my ear.

I kept mumbling for her to slow down because I couldn't remember everything. She just laughed throwing her head back with an ease that came from being long dead and on the other side. She looked exactly like she had in the picture of her and Annie when they were just a few years older than me. She smelled like sand after rain, salty ocean wind and green tomatoes still on the vine. Finally she stood up and everything became very quiet in the house. Her voice rang suddenly clear as she said:

"Don't you worry about Annie, she is with me now but listen close; you must bring all the elements together and free Morgan of the darkness. I have told you everything you need to know. Sleep now but remember that it is almost time to wake him up."

With that she turned and walked out the front door. As it slammed behind her I jolted awake aware that I now had a blanket covering me. I leapt from the chair and ran to the front door. When I swung it open I could still see the faint traces of foot prints leading up to the house in the snow. I stood there with the door open letting the cold sweep into the house cooling the feverish sensation that had enveloped me. It was like a burning inside my brain and my heart. It came with a feeling of intense power and purpose in what I needed to do in order to banish the entity once and for all. I wondered if Elsiba's element had been fire because the words she had whispered in my ear of spells and invocations felt burnt into my memory like a brand.

Locking the door behind me I made my way up to the turret room exhausted yet unable to sleep. The fiery power left behind by Elsiba was welling up inside of me making me restless. I rummaged through my bag and found the last of Father O'Malley's journals with the fake cover I had wrapped around it. With Margot's side of the story fresh in my mind and the confirmation that Malphus was indeed the same demon that inhabited both Father O'Malley and now Morgan, I opened the journal to read his final entries. It was the first moment of true calm that I had felt since I had arrived back in Port Townsend three and a half days ago.

As the snow covered town drifted to sleep, I read these final words.

October 31st, 1953

I am lost to the beast that is inside of me. Who I was and all the dreams and goodness that I once held close to my heart have been swallowed by the leviathan that rages in my mind. I know that it is too late for me and that I am forsaken. Father Benedict has tried his best and given his sweat and blood to remove the demon but it has been in vain and I know what I must do. I must kill the witch and the horror that she carries inside of her. The entity has told me that I will be fulfilling God's will by destroying this Jezebel and the forbidden knowledge that she carries in her blood and uses with an arrogance that displeases God and the Devil alike. It must end here with her and I will be God's sword and strike her down letting her blood flow until she is drained of life. It seems that I have been chosen to do this and while I flinch at the thought of bloodshed still I know that I will never be free until this deed is done.

Nov 1st, 1953

It is All Saints Day today and while my brothers light candles and sing hymns to the holy ones that are honored on this day I have asked St. George to help me slay the dragon that slithers in the body of the witch. She has no name to me anymore but rather is just the pure incarnation of evil and seduction that I will strike down in my obedience to God. May St. George stand at my side and give me the strength to see the action through to the end. The witch's husband leaves each morning for work at 7am sharp and she is left alone in that monstrosity of a house. I have found a place to hide overnight in the carriage house so as to watch the man leave and not to be suspected at the monastery of having gone missing. I will squat inside and listen to the movements of the night hidden away behind an old stack of apple crates that I have scouted out on my last visit to spy on the witch. This way, when the man's car pulls out of the property and she is left alone, I will only have to wait until she comes out back into her witch's garden for unholy herbs for her morning concoction. I have been watching all her movements and habits these past weeks and only once did the man catch me peeking in through the window but then it only made me more careful in my creeping. The nighttime is the ideal time to slip out of the monastery and hide in the carriage house listening to their words at the dinner table while watching the stars light up the black sky. When she comes outside tomorrow morning she will be mine. Malphus has told me that it must be tomorrow for it is the day when the lost souls go unprotected and I can kill the witch and her growing seed without worry of damnation. It must be tomorrow and now I am ready. Oh St. George fill me with your courage to strike down the evil in this woman as my offering to God.

Nov. 2, 1953

I know not what I have done but reading the words written only yesterday fill me with a humiliation that runs to my core. I awoke from this terrible madness in Margot Winship's kitchen holding a knife with all intent to murder this woman in cold blood. Her hair was tangled into a black nest of curls, her dress was torn and bloodied and her eyes looked like that of a wild animal as she shrieked a curse so powerful it nearly knocked me off my feet. The blows of the words alone are what have shaken me from the nightmare that has been the past few months although I now know what I must do. I am not meant for this earth and the only way to assure that no one will be destroyed by my wretched and possessed hand is to end my own life. I cannot live with the things that I have done and my poisoned brain is too weak to fight against my own darkness any longer. I have come to doubt whether or not there is an entity at all and that it has all been my own sick fabrication to veil my own dark desires. In this lucid moment I am taking the time to write this in the hopes that it will set Father Benedict's mind at ease that I am willingly going to take my own fetid life with no coercion. Margot's words spoke of a cursed death by water and I feel that her wishes must be carried forth immediately so *my innately cowardly self may not escape before her wish has been granted. The dark waters beckon to me and I will know no peace in the afterlife until I have somehow atoned for all my sins. I pray to you Lord that you may walk at my side and when the moment is ripe help my cursed soul to make amends.*

The last entry left me breathless as I saw only empty pages for the rest of the journal. What happened next I already knew from the newspaper clipping and the dream of his naked body swept out to sea, blue and lifeless. I felt a profound sadness fill me at his wasted and tortured life and all the pain that rippled outwards from this one cursed man. The entity was in him but in the end it seemed that he chose to end his life before he could end another's, which made me feel an empathy for this man that just a day ago would not have been possible. How I wished that Margot had read these journals all those years ago when Father Benedict had given them to Elsiba in the hopes that she would let go of her own hate. Would she have been able to forgive him? I wasn't sure but she would at least have known that in the end it was he who caused his own death and not her curse.

As I set the last journal back in my bag I knew that I would have to find a way to show Margot this last entry before she could burn this journal as she had the others. It was time to cleanse the family of the darkness that had been feeding on Morgan and Margot alike. And as I drifted off to sleep I knew that the first thing I would have to do would be to tell Deidre everything. I had to convince both she and Margot that it was time for us to join our strengths together and finish the removal and destruction of the entity once and for all -- not only for Morgan's sake but for our own as well. Elsiba had told me all I needed to know and I could feel her power surging through me like an electric current ready to bolt into action.

CHAPTER 27

Thursday morning arrived in a flash. As I lay still in my bed I noticed the wonderful sound of silence that only snow can bring to a modern town. There was a stillness that hung in the air and slowed everything down to a pace that would have been acceptable to the Winships of old. I forced myself to throw back the warm blankets and quickly get dressed in the morning chill that filled my room. I could tell that the house was empty and I imagined that Margot was already at the hospital watching over Morgan and controlling her grief over Annie's death as best she could. Pulling back the white curtains in my room I looked out over all the snow-covered roof tops and the completely enveloped streets. There wasn't a speck of anything that wasn't covered with at least six inches of fresh snow and it was still falling in thick, lazy flakes.

I made my way downstairs to the kitchen where I found one of George's old heavy flannel jackets waiting for me on my chair and a note from Margot telling me that she would be at the hospital until the evening. Grateful for the warm coat, I threw on my boots and not wanting to bother with driving in the fresh snow I began the walk over to Deidre's house. There is nothing like unexpected snow to bring out a more whimsical side of small town folk. As I walked in the beautiful powder I couldn't help but notice all the children and grownups alike who were also enjoying the mystery of this sudden burst of winter. I could see several fathers building snowmen with their children; a group of young boys ran past me with their sleds in tow, most likely on their way to the top of the steepest hill in town; and a group of toddlers making snow angels with their mother. I was even surprised to see Gladys and Bill Nelson cross country skiing on Tremont Street. In a way, Annie would have approved of all this childlike merriment.

As I rounded the corner to Adam's Street I could see my childhood home from the end of the block and was comforted in the fact that it hadn't changed a bit since I had left. Deidre's house was a two story Victorian that was long and thin and lined with holly trees on one side and a large garden on the other. It was a deep moss green color that made it look like it had simply grown up from out of the ground one night with its wooden spindles and leaf like lattice work on the covered front porch. There were two gabled windows that sat above the porch on the second story that from a distance looked like eyes with the front door being the nose and the walkway leading to the porch a smiling mouth. Hanging from the holly trees were at least thirty different handmade bird houses that the locals had given her over the years and the front porch had a dozen bird feeders clustered together.

As always the bird feeders were all a flutter with everything from common robins to chickadees and even a few hummingbirds feasting on the food that she had graciously left out for them in the sudden freeze. Like all Winships with their persistent green thumbs, the garden was filled to overflowing and being that it was mid-October it was an odd sight to see her huge pumpkin patch covered in snow. The orange orbs were peeking through the layer of white that had frozen them all overnight. Deidre had grown an impressive array of over fifty pumpkins all wound together in a jumble of tendrils and now crystalized leaves. I could already imagine the neighbor children's disappointment this year as Deidre wouldn't be able to create her usual Jack-o-lantern lined path to her door for all the trick-or-treaters. With her usual good humor and love of all things Halloween, she dressed up religiously as a witch each year telling Margot and I that "if you can't beat them then join them." It was after all only a few days before her and Morgan's birthday and the celebration would usually last the full three days until she couldn't even look at another piece of chocolate until the following year.

As I made my way up the front porch I came nose to nose with the tiniest of hummingbirds that hung in the air in front of me as if by a string. It fluttered its wings at a dizzying speed and began to squeak little tweeting noises at me.

"I'm not like her," I said to the little bird "I can't understand you." It hovered for a moment still and then realizing that I was not Deidre it plucked a piece of my hair out of my head and zipped away to tuck it in its nest. The front door was open as always. I called into the house while cleaning the snow from my wet boots.

"Are you upstairs?" I shouted as I hung my jacket on the coat rack. The entrance of the house was narrow as was typical of Victorian style. Directly in front of me was a long open staircase that led up to the two bedrooms on the second floor. To my immediate right was the parlor. Between the staircase and the parlor was a short hallway that opened into the kitchen and through the kitchen was a small glassed in sunroom which Deidre used for her plants.

"I'm up here," she called back and I knew that she was surely in what had been my old bedroom but was now her painting room. Deidre had always loved to paint but it wasn't until I had left home three years before that she really let herself indulge in her art. It had gotten to the point that if she wasn't in her shop or with Samir she was most certainly painting. She had started off with small square boards that she would cover with images of her bird friends and then it slowly grew into huge canvases that wove her vision of the town into a tapestry of color and whimsy.

As I climbed the steep stairwell and pushed open the door to her workroom I was greeting with a vision of Deidre in her paint splattered overalls. She was working on an eight by ten canvas that was framed with ancient trees, rows of little Victorian houses built on ground that was hollowed with images of saints and angels, like catacombs, and a snowy sky filled with crows. It was stunning in its size but also in the details that seemed to cover every inch of the massive canvas.

"How long have you been working on this?" I said, astonished that she ever had the time to create such intricate work.

"I started it last Friday and I should have known that it was a foreshadowing of sorts. I actually had to get out of bed to work on it because the images were keeping me awake at night," she said, as she wiped her paint brush on her pant leg. "Margot came to the hospital this morning and told me to come home for a while. I know I should be sleeping but I just can't."

"About Margot," I said, trying to find the words and the best place to begin with the story of Father O'Malley. "Last night, some things from the past surfaced and I think you need to know what is going on because I know what to do now to help Morgan."

Deidre stopped painting and turned to me with a look of surprise and confusion. "Go on," she said hesitantly. She set her brush down and instead turned to face me as I cleaned off a stool for a place to sit. I did the only thing I knew and simply started at the beginning and told her everything up until last night and my visit with Elsiba. I took the last of the journals out of my bag and handed it to her and watched as she quickly read the few pages that were left of his tortured thoughts.

Her hands shook as she read. In a rush all the blood had drained from her face leaving her an even paler white than usual. When she finished I began to tell her what we needed to do in order to set Morgan free. She listened nodding along with everything that I said and when I was finished I waited for her response hoping that she would say yes to what we needed to do despite the danger.

"I'll do it," she said almost breathlessly. "Let me deal with Margot but first we have Annie to tend to. I need to go to the funeral home in an hour and finish the details for the burial tomorrow. Can you open my store and tend shop for a few hours until I get everything settled? With all this snow there probably won't be anyone coming in but I really should open."

"Of course," I said, "and don't forget that Kat and Gavin are organizing the wake afterwards." She thought about that for a moment and then replied.

"Then that is when we will do it," she said. "The whole town will be at the bar and we won't have to worry about causing a stir with the ritual. I can't believe I am letting you do this."

"It has to be this way." I said, feeling like truer words had rarely left my lips. Everything had been building up to this for the past fifty years and it was time to set Morgan free. Deidre handed me the keys to her shop and as she showed me out the front door she took me in her arms with a force that startled me.

"I've missed you so much," she said and I could see that tears were threatening to well up in her eyes.

"I won't stay away anymore," I said, "I promise."

As I walked down the pathway back to the snow filled street I glanced behind me and saw Deidre standing on her porch with all the birds gathering to her with questioning looks as if asking her what was wrong. She threw a handful of seed into the snow but not even that could shake their worry as they all chirped and inched closer to her.

I waved and then began the walk to downtown not wanting to bother with going back for my car. As I made my way down the hill towards Water Street, the cheerful shouts of children filled the air with their unexpected joy at having a day off from school. By tomorrow afternoon we would be burying Annie in frozen soil and all the town adults would be warming their souls with a bit of ale in honor of her very long life. As I thought on this and the ritual that we would need to prepare for in order to free Morgan I noticed small footprints in the snow next to me. Like Deidre with her birds it seemed that I too had my own version of an uncommon yet concerned companion that wished to keep me company as I made my way through town.

CHAPTER 28

Before I began my life in Seattle, I spent all my afternoons in my mother's store "The Curious Crow" arranging artifacts, helping customers find their treasures and filling a small case with my own little amulet jewelry creations. Deidre had many gifts beyond speaking with birds and one of them was collecting the most unique objects the world of old had to offer. It was as if they called to her from under thick layers of dust hidden away in long forgotten attics. Sometimes I wondered if these pieces were trying to find their way to her as if they were more than just inanimate objects and sensed that she understood them like no one else could. She could hold an old skeleton key in her hand and tell me which house it came from or touch a Victorian mourning piece and tell me how the person had perished. It was only logical that she used this gift to make her living and people would come from all over the region to see her treasures as well as her wall of paintings.

Deidre's store was downtown on a little side street with a view of the water and a small beach below the pilings that held the little building above the tide's reach. Hanging from the old shiplap wood ceiling were the hundreds of antique glass fishing floats we had collected with Morgan. When the light would shine through the French windows each would come alive. The rainbows of their bottle green, frosty white and amber yellow shades created a swirl of color and light in the little shop. Wooden curio cabinets that had come from a mariner's museum in a neighboring fishing village housed every kind of trinket and treasure mostly from the Victorian era and earlier in fitting with the town. I would gaze for hours at the twinkling jewels that often caught the eyes of tourists and the baskets of old photographs and tin types that no longer had family to claim them. My mother would sit behind a large oak checkout stand with her long dark hair up in two braided buns. She pressed the old keys of her one hundred year-old cash register to ring out sales while as a child I played on the beach below.

Here I was again turning the key in the lock of the front door and flipping the closed sign to read open. I waved to Tobias as he was outside shoveling the snow off the sidewalk that ran along the front of his store. He made a little motion of lifting a coffee cup to his lips and I couldn't help but grin and shout across the street "yes please!" Switching on the lights I was thrilled to see that Deidre had a fresh basket of chopped wood waiting next to the standing Victorian wood stove. I quickly started a fire to warm up the freezing cold shop and began to turn on all the lights in the hope they would be a beacon to stranded tourists or curious town folk.

The door squeaked open, allowing Tobias to bring me a warm cup of coffee on a small platter.

"Good Morning, Miss Charlotte," he said with a twinkle in his eye. "I see you are back in the store."

"Yes, there are arrangements to be made for Annie," I said, hoping that he was already aware of her passing and that I would not have to be the harbinger of grave news.

"I thought as much," he said, looking suddenly weary as he placed my coffee on the check-out counter in front of me. "When I moved here, Annie was one of the first people who came in my shop." He said with a suddenly dreamy look in his eyes as if he was seeing that moment in time as clear as a photograph in his mind.

"I wish I had known Elsiba. She had long since passed when I was born," I said. "Will you come to the funeral tomorrow?"

"I will," he said while instinctively lowering his head as if saying a silent prayer. "Although at my age funerals do give a man reason for pause. It's too close..." His voice trailed off and I could feel a sudden presence in the room with us. Quickly I glanced to the door and his long dead wife June and son Hugo were standing patiently at the entrance to the store. "I best get over to the café in case there are people who need something to warm them up, eh! If you need anything just call over, ok dear."

As he hobbled out to the street the two ghosts followed dutifully behind him, their pale grey forms blending into the bright white of the snow covered ground. I sipped my coffee and looked out the wall of French windows that faced the bay. The water was so close to the bulk head as high tide began to roll in that I felt like I was in a boat instead of a building attached to pillars. The snow was coming down in a few small flakes now and with it a thin mist rose up from the water creating a gauzy veil. I walked closer to the windows where I had a view of the snow covered beach along with the deeper water. Looking down into the lazy waves I spied several seals peering up at me.

Kat, Gavin and I had made this small patch of waterfront our playground and the seals would always try to flop onto shore to play with us. Curious and unafraid of humans they would inch their way closer as we built our sandcastles and skipped rocks. Gavin often teased me that our favorite seal, who was marked with a white ribbon-like stripe around his body, had fallen in love with me and wanted to take me home as his bride. Today, watching those round black eyes staring up at me, I couldn't help but think of the story Elsiba had told Margot about her own father's death at sea. It seemed that as I got closer to discovering the truth about my families' past more secrets emerged.

A few children began to congregate on the small beach bundled up in so many layers of clothes they could barely put their arms down. I waved to them and they smiled and went back to making snowballs and screeching with delight completely unaware of what had brought the sudden chill to town. Settling back down on my chair I was immediately overcome with the strangest sensation of something powerful approaching. The shop filled with the sudden scent of oranges and burning candles. I ran to check on the stove fearing a flue fire but it was crackling away normally and all the hinges were set properly. The smell was so intense that it made my head begin to spin and I couldn't help but ask out loud:

"Annie, is that you?" I whispered, but I knew she was not there. It was something else that I did not recognize as being friend or foe but rather just immensely powerful. I noticed the children outside began to scream louder with what sounded like fear. Quickly I ran to the door and stepped out onto the small wooden deck that was perched over the beach in time to see them all furiously throwing snowballs out at the water. Thinking they were throwing them at the seals I rushed to the edge of the porch to scold them but was stopped immediately in my tracks as two figures glided across the water in the mist.

I could barely believe my eyes as the two men with their Stetson hats perched neatly on their heads walking calmly and in synch across the water towards us. The snowballs that the children were throwing began to get perilously close to the two men as they strolled across the water's surface. Their faces were expressionless while the children were becoming increasingly frenzied in their throwing until one of the older children turned and ran back towards the street. Eventually the others ran laughing behind him.

As "the Strangers" continued their approach the seals quickly dove below the surface and I could feel their power pulsing around me. I stood motionless, freezing in the snow, not knowing if I should run or face them although they seemed to have yet to notice me. A loud dog bark on the street caught my attention as a large black Labrador out for a walk with his master began jumping and barking wildly toward the beach. In the time it took for me to turn my head to the dog and then back to the water "the Strangers" had vanished as suddenly as they had appeared.

I backed my way into the shop, chilled to the bone. It took several minutes before the dog had calmed down and I was able to feel the blood coming back into my fingers and toes. The overwhelming feeling of the unknown presence made me queasy with fear as my adrenaline began to wane. I stood by the warm stove scanning the bay but the figures were entirely gone and all that was left was the mist and the last of the snowflakes trickling down.

As the hours passed and I began to recover from the shock of seeing "the Strangers" my mind went back and started to hit on several of the details that Margot had mentioned last night. If Morgan had made some type of a deal with these creatures in order to remove the dark entity from his soul, what had he promised in return? Had he promised the souls of the earth bound ghosts that filled all the empty attics and dank cellars in this forgotten town? Did these creatures prey on the dead and the living alike? And why was it that children could see them as clearly as I could? All these questions swirled in my mind as the hours ticked by and customers wandered in and out of the store. Whatever they were tomorrow night during the coming ritual I had a feeling we would find out once and for all.

CHAPTER 29

The sun was setting fast as I locked the door after the last customer had left toting their bag of curious new treasures. I had spent the day looking over my shoulder out at the water while trying to act normal in front of the few tourists who had wandered in as they were unable to leave town for the snow. There was no sign of "the Strangers" although it took hours for the smell of oranges to leave the store. More interesting was the fact that I was not alone in smelling the rich perfume as almost everyone commented on how wonderful the shop smelled. One woman even demanded that I show her where our candle section was because she could smell them the minute she had entered the room.

I heard a light rapping on the glass door and turned in time to see Deidre and Samir standing outside looking cold and pale. Letting them in they dusted off the snow from their jackets and both quickly headed to the small wood stove that was still crackling away with its warm flame.

"It took longer than we thought to make all the arrangements for tomorrow's service," said Deidre as she shivered trying to slowly warm her body. "Annie had everything already planned out years ago but there were still quite a few details that needed tending to."

"Has Margot gone home?" I asked, wondering how she was holding up with the stress of Annie's death on top of everything else.

"She is still at the hospital and wanted to know if you were coming by or if I should take this shift?" Deidre said in a soft voice. I could tell that she was tired and most likely needed to rest.

"I'll go if you want to get some sleep and come by later tonight," I volunteered hoping she would go home and sleep for at least a few hours. I could tell she was running on nerves and soon would slip into exhaustion with the stress of the funeral. She was silent for a moment and I could tell that while she wanted desperately to lay her head down for a bit she also didn't want to place the burden on me.

"Really, I don't mind. I'm not tired and Tobias brought me a huge sandwich this afternoon so I've eaten and can last until at least midnight," I said, hoping she would take me up on my offer.

"Alright then, I'll go get some sleep and I will be back to the hospital by midnight. Also most of the town will be closing their shops for the funeral tomorrow," she said while Samir put his arm around her. We talked about the sales at the shop and while I wanted to tell her about "the Strangers" I still felt that she should tell Samir on her own. So instead we talked about Annie's funeral preparations and Morgan's unchanged condition.

"I will be back at the hospital later tonight for my rounds," said Samir, "so if you are tired I will be there making sure all is well." The thought of his being there comforted me even if it was just to know that I was not alone in those white halls watching helplessly over Morgan.

We eventually turned off all the lights, totaled out the till and let the fire burn down to cold embers before locking the door for the night. The mist that hung on the water was still floating near the beach and I could hear the seals splashing in the lazy waves that were rolling in. Snow drifts had quietly accumulated all day long leaving a thick coating of what looked like icing on all the buildings. It was as if the turrets and spires were part of a large wedding cake that twinkled in the fading light.

Samir gave me a ride back to the Winship house where I barely managed to back my car out of the driveway and slowly made my way across the thick layer of ice that had settled on all the roads. By the time I got to the hospital I had almost slid into a ditch twice and managed to delicately glide into a parking spot in the hospital visitor's lot. As I walked through the familiar sliding doors and down the long corridors I could hardly believe that at nearly the same time yesterday I had been running through these same halls in shock and panic over Annie's death. And that tomorrow we would be having her funeral. It still all felt like a horrible dream and I couldn't shake myself awake.

Margot was sitting in our usual plastic chair with her head hung staring at her clasped hands. Even from a distance I could see that her eyes were rimmed in red and that she had worn herself out with grief. She lifted her head to look at me as I made my way closer.

Rising slowly she pulled me into her arms with an urgency that left me breathless. I didn't know what to say so I just held her and listened as she whispered little prayers under her breath not wanting to let me go. I knew that I would need to tell her about the ritual tomorrow night but I couldn't seem to find the words.

"Don't worry," I said lamely, "everything will be as it is meant to be."

She slowly let me go and looked at me with a sudden twinkling in her eyes. "You sounded just like my Mother Elsiba just then," she said with a tight smile.

Before I even knew what I was saying it all came out in one big rush. I told her about the visit from Elsiba during the night and how she had told me of the steps that we must take to set Morgan free. I told her how it had to be the three of us together combining all our gifts and power to bring forth the fire that would cleanse the entity from his soul.

"It's too dangerous. I know more about these things than you may think and I cannot risk losing you and your mother as well as Morgan. We have already lost Annie." Her voice choked and I felt a wave of despair wash over me. It was not going to be as simple as I had hoped but I refused to give up. Being a Winship I knew that one of my strengths was sheer stubbornness.

As Margot gathered her purse from the chair and bundled herself up in her winter coat I noticed that the snow was starting to fall once again outside. I knew that I should be thinking of Annie and all that was to come in the morning but I couldn't help but feel that there was still a chance to save Morgan and break this terrible curse that had fallen on our family. How could I just go on with my life if there was a way to help Morgan and I didn't convince Margot to at least try? The alternative of letting him waste away was unimaginable.

"Get yourself home soon. I'll leave something for you to eat in the oven. We have a sad day to come tomorrow," she said as she left me to stay with Morgan. Watching her walk down the hall I noticed that she had left her long hair loose and flowing down her back. It was still raven black at her age but with one long white stripe that started at her temple and left a white streak through the long wavy strands of hair. She usually wore it up in a braided bun but today she simply hadn't bothered to attach it. It was undoubtedly another sign of her sorrow.

I was alone again in the quiet hallway with the dark creatures peeking around corners at me and occasionally knocking over trays or other precariously placed items. It was always best to ignore them so in order to do that I decided to examine yet again the strange burns that covered Morgan's inert body. Nothing had changed since I had arrived and he had been placed in this tiny room with the glass window keeping the infections out. The burns moved in such a strange scale-like pattern that he almost looked like a sea creature that had been regurgitated from the deepest fathoms of the ocean floor; blind and without pigment. Even his toes had the patterned burns and on closer inspection it seemed that as he would breathe the scales would ripple and expand as if something parasitic was moving just under the skin.

Of course I knew that there was a parasite hovering over him at all times waiting for him to die in order to move on to the next victim. Not knowing how to convince Margot that we needed to join together to bind this entity once and for all, I began to think on ways to persuade her. Looking through the glass I noticed the small star birthmark on Morgan's shoulder and it struck me how it looked exactly like two triangles overlapping one another. It was as if someone had taken the very symbols that I had seen in his hidden book just yesterday and drawn them onto his shoulder one upside down and the other right side up. The symbol was familiar as being the combination of all the elements. It was odd to think that from the very beginning of his life he had been marked with the symbol that would represent the key to unlocking the entities grip on him.

The more I stood there looking at the marks the more I noticed that the entity was expanding through the room. It was a huge shadow that emptied into all the corners, silently filling the space accompanied with a feeling of unease. Like a giant spider unfolding its legs, the darkness was shifting through the room and I couldn't help but feel that it was watching me. It already had Morgan in its web but I was just on the periphery becoming a possible threat to its survival so it was observing my movements. I kept my eyes on Morgan not wanting to let

Malphus see my fear as the dark shadows started to form into different shapes that I could make out from the corner of my eye.

It was taunting me, daring me to look at it and while I felt fear filling my body there was also another sensation that began to bubble up inside of me. It was anger. Anger that Annie had been taken from us and anger that Morgan had suffered countless years of his life trying to fight this darkness from the inside out. The anger made me feel suddenly stronger. As I looked straight into the gathering darkness I spoke out loud to the demon that was squatting inside of Morgan like nothing more than a tape worm.

"I know your name now. You can't have him," I said, exuding all my energy and power at the entity. Before I could understand what was happening I was flying through the air with glass exploding around my body and a flock of crows rushing at me. The entity had blown all the glass out of the window that had separated us and had split itself into a hundred crows that cawed and pecked at me as I was thrown against the far wall from the power of the blast. The impact with the wall knocked all the breath from my body. I hit the ground gasping and curled my limbs into a ball to protect myself from the crows prying beaks. I could hear footsteps running down the hall towards me and Samir's familiar voice scream out my name.

He lifted me up from the ground and as I struggled to stand I saw that my shirt was covered in blood and there were a million shards of glass at my feet. The crows were gone and I could hear others running to see what had caused such a horrific noise in the otherwise silent hospital. Doctors rushed to check on Morgan and began to take measures to protect his already fragile body. In the melee Samir herded me into an empty room and immediately began to inspect my wounds.

"What was that Charlotte?" he said with an unusual tone of fear in his voice. Nothing ever seemed to frighten or surprise him so to hear that from him made me come around even faster. My head was throbbing. While the little pieces of glass had left small gashes all over me, the majority of the blood had come from a large cut on my forehead that was gushing.

"What did you see?" I asked, feeling nauseous with the sudden trauma.

"When I came around the corner I saw you fly through the air as the window exploded and," he paused for a moment almost as if he couldn't believe what he was about to say, "there were hundreds of crows that came swarming out of Morgan's room attacking you. But when I got to you the crows had disappeared."

"I think you need to talk to Deidre about this," I said, feeling ill with the sight of so much of my own blood. "She can tell you everything."

As he called in a nurse and began to clean out the gash and prepare to stitch up the wound, I could see that he was visibly shaken by what he had seen. One of the nurses told us that Morgan had been moved to another observation room and that there must have been a problem with one of the oxygen tanks to cause such a strange explosion. Of course I knew what had really caused the explosion but I just shook my head and let them work on putting me back together again like a rag doll. As I lay there feeling the tug of the needle pull my skin together I knew that logically I should have been terrified of what had just happened but instead I felt a wave of calm wash over me. In a moment of clarity I had the deepest realization that Malphus was the one who was afraid of me.

Chapter 30

Curled up in one of the empty hospital beds, I tried my best not to move my head. The throbbing in the freshly stitched wound was accompanied by a piercing pain. I should have called James today but I just couldn't think of how to even begin to tell him any, or all, that had been happening here without sounding completely insane or breaking down into a blubbering mess. Just knowing that he would be here soon filled me with a terrible anxiety as I realized that I longed for him to know all there was about me but feared his rejection most of all. I felt miserable all of a sudden caught between the simple life I had fashioned in Seattle and the haunting reality that was always just under the surface. Tomorrow the two would finally meet and either James would accept me and my strange gifts, or he would act as so many others had in the past with fear and inevitable rejection.

As I lay in the cool bed, above the covers, on my side facing the door I knew that Morgan was just on the other side of the wall. He had been moved to a new observation room and while I couldn't be keeping guard in the hall for all the dizziness, I still felt like I was close enough to run into the hall if something horrible came to pass. Through the walls Malphus' presence was pulsating. I had the feeling that if I put my hand on the wall I would feel the plaster beating like a heart. Samir had given me a pain killer and it had made everything a bit softer around the edges but there was still pain and consciousness to contend with as I lay motionless, thinking. My thoughts jumped between James, Annie, Morgan, Father O'Malley, Malphus and "the Strangers" like a bizarre play list of characters from past and present combined into a grotesque theatre. Overall I knew that I was bordering on exhaustion but more than that Malphus had been betting that a physical trauma would stop me from moving ahead with the ritual. If Samir hadn't arrived when he did it could have been much worse but thankfully his presence had broken the hex that Malphus had flung at me in its attempt to put an end to any talk of removing him from

Morgan.

As midnight approached the dark beings became more active in their wanderings, shadows moved across the half lit walls and odd noises could be heard just under the hush of the hospital ventilation system. It was a relief when Deidre came rushing into the room with Samir behind her. I had made him promise to let her sleep and come as planned. He was reluctant but eventually agreed. She was by my side in a flash and the worry lines were a mess of creases as she sat on the edge of the bed to better inspect my wounds. If she had been a mother cat she would have been licking my cuts and bruises but instead she peered under bandages and frantically asked Samir and I questions. I knew it was time for her to tell Samir all that was going on. Feeling weak with the blood loss and psychic assault I told her all that had happened not caring that Samir was standing there taking it all in. His face had gone from his usual caramel color to an ashen grey as he heard the demon's name.

"It is time we told him everything," I finally said to Deidre and while I could tell that a part of her didn't want to verbalize all that had come to pass in the end she let out a sigh and told Samir to pull up a chair. She told him everything that had happened the past four days from Malphus, to the priestly visits and finally to the arrival of "the Strangers." I filled in the blanks and told them of the morning visitation of "the Strangers" who had crossed the bay in the mist for an unknown purpose. As I spoke in a soft voice not wanting to make the throbbing pain in my head any worse I could tell that my words had triggered something in Samir. His eyes looked troubled as if he was grasping at a memory that was just on the periphery of his mind. When Deidre and I had finished the three of us sat silent for a moment the words still hovering in the air like the smoke from a snuffed candle.

I heard Samir clear his throat as Deidre and I waited for some type of a reaction from him. He had been in our lives long enough to know that unusual things tended to happen in our midst but the events of the past few days had surpassed everything up to this point. Finally he began to speak, his words echoing off the white walled room.

"When you said 'the Strangers' it gave me an odd nagging feeling that reminded me of something I had heard somewhere before.

It took a few minutes for it to come to me," he said while leaning back in his chair. "My mother told me a story about how she and my great grandmother were traveling on a pilgrimage to Northern Iran to visit the Mosque in Esfahan. This was in the 1950s and it was a tradition for people to go to this holy site in order to pay homage. As they made their way by bus there was a sudden torrential rain that hit the region and caused intense flooding. I know many were killed and my Mother said that she remembers the water rising inside the bus while they sat there trapped.

As you know my mother is quite petite and her mother was even smaller than she at no more than 4 feet and 9 inches tall. They knew that if they got out of the bus they would be swept away in the current. On the road hundreds of people were stepping into the muddy rapids as the buses were completely overwhelmed by water. This is when a very odd thing occurred. Two men appeared on the bus as if out of thin air. My mother described them as being exceptionally tall and wearing all white clothing. The one man she said had a strangely marked face and they took both my mother and Grandmother and carried them through the water for miles. They walked for at least 8 hours waist deep in water following in a long line of people who had been lucky enough not to drown in the floods. They barely spoke. The men in white gave one another conspiratorial looks that marked a conversation without words.

They ended up carrying them all the way to the high steps of the Mosque where they would be safe and taken care of until the waters retreated. My Grandmother and Mother thanked them and offered them gifts if they would give their names and addresses. The men simply smiled and shook their heads refusing any reward. As they turned to enter into the Mosque they both realized that the two men had vanished as if they had never been there to begin with. But the thing that struck me was that many people on the road saw them especially the children and because the men were so unusually tall for the region and also had light skin they had taken to calling them the 'farangi'."

Deidre and I looked at each other not knowing what the word meant and waiting for Samir to go on.

"This word 'farangi' means 'stranger' in Farsi."

I held my breath as the meaning of the word began to sink into my tired mind. Deidre gasped but Samir held up his hand in a gesture that meant he had not yet finished.

"But there is more, these 'farangi' or 'strangers' had saved both my Mother and my Grandmother and in doing so also saved the child that my Mother was carrying inside of her. That is how my brother got the nickname 'Mal'ak' which means 'angel' because my Mother and Grandmother were convinced that the two men were not men at all but rather two Guardian angels come to save them."

Deidre and I were both stunned into silence by Samir's story. It had occurred to me before that "the Strangers" may not be something menacing; however, the feeling that came with them was of such overwhelming power it was hard not to immediately feel fear. I never felt fear when a ghost would make itself known. Even the dark entity that clung to Morgan made me feel dread at being in its presence but I still felt like I could hold my own against it. The same was not so of "the Strangers" in the sense that their power radiated from them in a way that made me positive that if they chose to they could squash me like a bug. That was where the fear came into the picture, whether or not it was a rational response was another question altogether.

One thing I had become certain of was that Morgan had called them here and it seemed like they were waiting for something to come to pass. All I could do now was trust that they would play a part in the ritual that would come tomorrow at dusk and hope that it would be in helping us. Deidre and Samir were whispering in the corner as I drifted in and out of sleep. Far away in my mind I could hear the words Margot would say when I was a child as we knelt by the bedside saying our prayers. "Now I lay me down to sleep, I pray the Lord my soul to keep, and if I die before I wake, I pray the Lord my soul to take." The drugs had begun to have their effect and my limbs were suddenly heavy.

Before I knew it Samir was helping me into the Winship house with Margot at the front door choking back sobs at seeing the gash on my head. He had driven me home although I couldn't remember leaving the room or walking to the car or his driving for that matter. He helped me up the three flights with Margot following close behind questioning him about what had happened. As I fell into the softness of my bed I closed my eyes and listened to them speak in rushed whispers. The word "crow" rolled off Samir's tongue with an intonation that had become so familiar yet foreign all the same. After he left with a kiss on my forehead and a hug for Margot I tried for a moment to get out of my bed and reach for my bag as Samir had dutifully left it hanging on the chair.

Margot was immediately at my side as I crumbled back into the pillows and gestured for her to bring me the purse. She sat at my side as I lay there fumbling through the detritus that filled it: brush, wallet, lipstick, business cards in their silver holder, notebook, mints, and finally Father O'Malley's last journal. I un-wrapped the book sleeve from the outside that I had used to cover it and handed it to her.

"No more secrets. Please don't burn it before you can read it. Please," I said in a pleading voice that came from my now uninhibited mind thanks to the pain killers. "We have to do the ritual tomorrow. I know what to do but it cannot happen without all three of us."

She looked at the journal I had placed in her hands with annoyance and I could tell that she was wondering if the fire downstairs was still burning high enough to consume the evil missile. I reached out and touched her hand and noticed that despite how thin her skin had become that our hands had the same size and shape. It took the last of my energy to say to her before drifting into a drug induced sleep:

"Say the bedtime prayer for me."

Letting out a long sigh she covered me with my blanket tucking me in tight as she had when I was a child. Her withered yet beautiful hands switched off the light and she said the words which sounded like the most powerful of protection spells on her lips. The door clicked shut and Margot's slow steps began the descent into the kitchen. In the dark I drifted off to sleep with wild dreams of owls tapping on my window and Elsiba and Annie playing 1930s jazz on the phonograph in the parlor downstairs.

CHAPTER 31

The clock showed 8 a.m. as I opened my eyes after a night of drugged sleep. The light outside the window was bright with the glow of snow glimmering on every surface. Hanging on the open door to my closet like a harbinger of despair was the black dress that I had packed. Margot had pressed it for me knowing that today it would be put to use at Annie's funeral. It was strange to think that only a few days earlier I had made the frantic journey back home thinking it would be for Morgan's burial only to have things become even more complex than I could ever have imagined.

As I lifted my head from the pillow a sudden wave of dizziness came over me although the pain was all but gone. I slowly pulled myself up, sore and aching from being thrown into a wall the night before by Malphus, and quietly made my way down to the kitchen. My stomach was rumbling with hunger and as I started down the stairs I could already smell coffee brewing and warm toast waiting for me.

Margot was busy in the kitchen cleaning off the old candles from Annie's memorial altar. She was scraping off the old wax and saving it in a little pouch to melt back down later for a new candle. A glass of rose water sat at the Madonna's feet and there were new bouquets surrounding the pictures of Annie and all the other small relics that were carefully arranged.

"Coffee is ready and toast is on the table," she said, gesturing to my usual spot which was laid out with a plate of toast and Bee's honey. Margot always had a knack for knowing when someone would be coming to her table and as she had gotten older her timing was tuned to perfection. The toast was just up and the coffee was steaming in my mug. My throat felt dry, which was surely a side effect from the pain killers, and while the toast scratched in my mouth the warm flood of coffee that followed was absolute bliss.

"The funeral is at 2 p.m. so there is no hurry if you want to just stay here and rest," she said while lighting the newly arranged candles. "I am going to the hospital and Deidre will come to pick you up around 1:30 since your car is still parked there."

I nodded my agreement, as my mouth was too full to politely respond. I knew that we would have to do the ritual tonight but I didn't know how to try to breach the subject again. The kitchen was silent with only the stove crackling and as I looked out the window into the snow-filled yard I noticed that the flakes had finally stopped falling. Margot looked weak with grief and yet stronger than she been yesterday. Ever since I had left three years before I had in some way been preparing myself for Annie's passing. Her hourglass had run so much longer than most with her joy and courage in living a simple and beautiful life. In many ways I was thankful that she had not come to me with regrets or secrets after she had passed. It meant that she was peaceful and had moved on with a grace and dignity that fit her so very well. So while my sadness ran deep at her moving on it was also tinged with pride that I had been a part of her family in practice although not in name.

After lighting all the candles Margot sat with me at the table sipping her coffee while watching the wicks flicker with tiny lights. Outside the town was quiet with even more snow to contend with than the day before and a coming funeral that most would try to attend in one way or another. There would be a memorial in the funeral home, followed by a ceremony by the grave site where Annie would be put to rest in the Winship tomb next to Elsiba, and finally a wake afterwards at the bar which would last well into the small hours of the night.

"I feel like I am losing my mother all over again," she said while holding her cup in both hands for its warmth and comfort.

"I can only imagine," I said, feeling at a loss for the words that would give relief from the pain that was holed up inside of her. Slowly she raised her eyes to mine and said "I will do the ritual."

My heart fluttered with sudden excitement and relief despite my calm demeanor. Not knowing how to reply I again just nodded my head. I wondered if she had read Father O'Malley's last entries of regret and clarity and had made her decision afterwards. Or if the attack on me by Malphus had convinced her that we would never really be safe until this entity was bound and gone. Whatever had changed her mind I didn't want to swing her back in the other direction, so I sat there quietly with her, feeling the cold air through the window pane.

"We should start as the sun begins to set," I said, lifting my eyes to meet hers. "It is best if we make an appearance at the wake and then quietly slip out around 6 p.m."

"Do we need to bring anything?" she said with a hint of nervousness in her voice.

"No. Just you, Deidre and I need to be there and then we will call on the beings of light to help us in our endeavor. Let's hope they show up," I said.

Margot gathered up her jacket and giving me a long hug she left out the mud room door. Her car rumbled to life as she slowly backed out of the snow-filled driveway and made her way to Morgan's side at the hospital. Sitting in the still of the house I wondered what James was doing right this minute. I closed my eyes and imagined him already in his office with the phone tucked under his chin talking to clients as he sketched and riffled through papers. Just thinking about him brought the first smile to my face that I had felt in days.

Picking up the phone I called his office hoping to not have to talk to his secretary who was nice enough but always chattier than I cared for. His voice sounded through the receiver amid a rustle of papers in the background.

"It's me," I said in a tiny voice that sounded scratchy and childlike to my ears.

"Charlotte, I called five times last night!" he shrieked into the phone. Another wave of guilt washed over me as I had all but forgotten him in the chaos. "I had a horrible feeling last night that something was terribly wrong. I just couldn't shake it and so I called Margot's house but no one answered."

"I'm so sorry, James," I said, feeling horrible that he had been worried and also intrigued that he had sensed that something was amiss. He never said things like that so this was new to me. "It has been an intense couple of days. Annie passed away and the funeral is today."

"Oh Charlotte, I'm so sorry," he said, suddenly lowering his voice as all his anger and worry suddenly evaporated. Even though he knew little about the Winship reputation in town I had told him about all the people that I loved and had known my whole life. He knew about Annie Christy and Bee. He had met Margot and Deidre on the rare occasions when they had come to Seattle to visit. And I had even told him about old Tobias Gunn and countless others. He knew that Annie was like family to us. "Do you need me to leave work and come now?"

I felt a sudden wave of panic at the thought of him being here when we had to go forward with the ritual tonight.

"No, it is fine. Even if you left now it would be too late for the service," I said, hoping that would persuade him to continue his day as planned. "Also there has been a snow storm here and I don't know what the roads are like coming over so you may want to wait until tomorrow."

"I know! It is all everyone is talking about here. The sudden snow on the peninsula! If you listen to the news casters they make it sound like it's the end of the world," he said and I could almost see the little smirk on his lip. "I'll come tonight."

"If I am not at the house than I am at the wake which is in Kat and Gavin's bar. You can find me there," I said, hoping that I wasn't setting us both up for disaster. If the ritual went as planned then all would be well but if it went horribly wrong then he would be walking right into the eye of the storm.

"Are you sure you don't want to wait until its daylight to come over," I said, trying desperately to convince him to stay away one more day.

"I miss you Charlotte. I want to be there with you and your family. Don't worry, I will be fine and if there is a problem I'm sure I can handle it," he said and I hoped that he was right.

"I'll see you tonight," I said, and then added "I love you," meaning it with all my heart and hoping that it wasn't the last time that I would hear him respond in kind.

"I love you too," he said and then hung up. The dial tone rang in my ear for a minute until I finally hung up as well and made my way back upstairs. The only place I wanted to be was in bed under the covers were I felt safe and warm. Everything was silent. As I lay there hiding in my refuge of pillows and handmade quilts piled high I began to plot each step of the ritual like practicing a dance routine in my mind. To bring everything together in perfect synchronicity could be done but I could only pray that "the Strangers" were there to help and not to destroy us entirely.

CHAPTER 32

The funeral home was built on the outskirts of Port Townsend as if having it within the town limits carried some sort of ill will towards the living. As Deidre and I walked into the main room the smell of open white lilies filled the space with a rich perfume so intoxicating that it made my head spin. The small room was full not only of hundreds of bouquets of flowers but also with a large number of people from town who had known Annie most of their lives. Margot was seated in the front row on one of the old wooden benches. They were lined up in neat rows like an old church and the casket was open giving people a last chance to see dear old Annie.

As I made my way up the aisle I could hear people begin to whisper to each other. I wondered if they were talking about the fact that I had found Annie. Or maybe they were chattering about Morgan and the ruckus that had gone on in the hospital the night before. Whatever it was I tried my best to ignore it and focus on paying my respects to the departed. Sitting in the front row I slipped in next to Margot and she whispered in my ear that Samir was keeping a close eye on Morgan until we could get back now that he knew what was going on.

As people kept filtering in and out of the room Margot finally walked to the front of the room and stood at the small pulpit that was just to the side of Annie's coffin. As she looked out over the crowd everyone became suddenly quiet as her presence in any situation demanded attention and respect. She cleared her throat and with trembling hands looked up to the crowd and began to speak.

"Today we are all here to lay Annie Christy to rest. She was the last of the pioneers and one of the reasons why we can call this rugged part of the earth our town and our home. She came out west seeking freedom and adventure and when she landed here, young and full of wonder; she told me that she had found her place in the world. I can only hope that she has now found her place in heaven and that angels have guided her home in winged chariots. I know that she would not want us to weep at her passing but rather to rejoice in the beauty that was her life. She never faltered when friends needed a helping hand, she always held her door open to those in need and never a more honest soul has lived in these woods. She was a mother to me and a Grandmother to all of us. May we never forget her and may the story of her life live on forever in the minds of our children and generations to come. I invite you to step forward to speak about Annie and her life and in doing so honor her memory."

One by one people took turns telling stories and little anecdotes about Annie and her young antics all the way to the more recent stories of her attempts to still drive despite her near blindness. Paul Jepson laughed that she had nearly run him off the road once in her old jalopy but since it only went about twenty miles an hour tops it was all rather humorous. Janette Frye remembered when she came by trick or treating at the Winship house and Annie, already well into her 80s, had answered the door wearing an old lady mask as her costume. Luke Hennely told of when he and his family had fallen on hard times and Annie had split enough wood for them and herself to last through winter and never asked for a thing in return. Carmine Perlotta recounted some of their wild nights in the old town tavern when Annie played cards with the men and could drink them all under the table. Old Gus remembered Annie going to work in the fields. She would show up so drunk that they would tie her onto the tractor seat so she wouldn't fall off. Frank Bishop told of how frightened he was when as a child he first saw Annie drive into town with a dead bob cat tied to the hood of her model-T. By the end of the funeral everyone was wearing an odd combination of wistful smiles and glistening eyes.

We headed the procession to the graveyard for the burial. Standing in the deep snow the coffin that held Annie's age torn body was gently placed next to Elsiba's in the Winship tomb. As each person dropped a single white lily on Annie's grave and proceeded to shake Margot and Deidre's hands, I decided to walk in the graveyard and take a moment of quiet for myself. Images of Annie's long life swirled in my mind as my own tears began to fall now that I was out of sight of any onlookers. The snow gathered into odd shapes on the black tombstones giving the impression of walking in a black and white photograph. The colors had all drained away with the white snow blinding me like a saturated flash of light.

My legs were almost numb as I had worn my black dress with boots laced high and an old black jacket Deidre had lent me. Ignoring the cold that nipped at my skin I wandered farther into the older side of the cemetery that had been all but abandoned over the years. This was the Catholic side that belonged to the monastery. Some of the graves were being uprooted by the willow and lilac trees leaving cracked marble shards rising from the ground. As I stepped through the many broken tombs I noticed a movement by one of the weepiest of willow trees ahead of me.

At first I thought it was a frozen branch that had moved in the wind. Then I saw the grey man's face peeking around the side of the tree trunk watching me. He had a wide smile on his face and at first I wasn't sure if he was alive or one of my ghosts as everything had taken on a shade of grey in the snow covered landscape. But the familiar tingle on the back of my neck and his odd movements confirmed that this was a ghost and he wanted to show me something.

I approached him slowly. As I got closer he slipped from behind the tree and motioned for me to follow. He was wearing a priest's black robes. His white hair proved that he had been an old man when he had died. We walked this way for a while with me about 10 feet behind him at all times as we wove our way farther into the oldest parts of the cemetery. Some of the tombstones were from the first settlers while others were mixed in all the way to the 1950s depending on the family. As we turned into a small alcove of the graveyard near another large willow the ghost stopped and pointed at a gravestone with an odd but friendly smile. I didn't want to approach closer while he was standing. He was persistently motioning to the grave insisting that I examine it. I inched my way closer keeping him in view the whole time. My eyes quickly darted to the name carved on the tomb leaving my breath caught somewhere in my frozen chest. I looked back to the priest expecting him to be near. Instead he had retreated at least ten tombstones from where I was although he was still watching me as I inspected the stone. It read in old gothic letters:

HERE LIES FATHER BENEDICT CALLAHAN
JUNE 20ᵀᴴ 1878 — JANUARY 4ᵀᴴ 1956

The name registered immediately in my mind as it was the priest that had tried desperately to help Father O'Malley free himself from the entity. The same man who had given the journals to Elsiba in the hopes of helping Margot come to terms with the attack and the circumstances of his tragic death. As I kneeled down to look closer at the old grave I noticed the edges of writing peeking up from under the drifts of snow. I began to brush the settled flakes off the tomb. Below his name and date of birth and death was a quotation written in a scrolling text that took up the bottom half of the tombstone.

ALWAYS BE HOSPITABLE TO STRANGERS
LEST THEY BE ANGELS IN DISGUISE —YEATS

My head shot up to look for him. He was motionless under the willow. With a smile on his face he nodded to me and then raised his hand in a farewell gest before fading into the tree. The words ran through my brain with a fire that left me reeling with an epiphany that had been building up to this moment for days. The nagging feeling that had begun to invade my thoughts that "the Strangers" may be some type of angelic force was yet again being confirmed. This was the man who had taught Margot that magic came to women from their angelic lovers. This was also the man who knew Elsiba well and now here he was showing me these words that he had found so dear they had been inscribed on his grave stone.

I began to rush through the old tombs trying to find my way back to the fresh dirt of Annie's grave. I tripped over the old stones and slipped through the sheets of ice that lay just under the snow. My mind raced as I began to understand how "the Strangers" would play their role in the liberation of Morgan's soul tonight.

CHAPTER 33

In all the years that I had lived in Port Townsend I had participated in more funerals that I could possibly begin to count which inevitably left the town traditions well engrained. It wasn't until I went to Seattle and was part of a city funeral that I realized how different it was from what I had experienced my entire life. When James' uncle passed away after having an unexpected heart attack, I sat in the church pews holding on tightly to James' hand both to give him comfort and also to steady my own nerves. I expected his uncle's ghost to come looking for me during the service wondering why he had died so suddenly. Thankfully nothing of the like came to pass and instead I found myself observing the very formal rituals that were taking place in a calm demeanor. The priest did not allow members of the family to speak, the casket was closed and everyone argued with me that a wake was held before the funeral instead of afterwards although no one cared for them anymore so rarely did a wake occur. For the first time I felt like a small town girl unfamiliar with the accepted social norms surrounding death.

This is not to say that there wasn't the same depth of sadness at losing a loved one in the city; however, the expression of that loss was so much more introverted than I was accustomed to viewing. In Port Townsend, when a member of the community died there was a very specific ritual that followed which included the ceremony, either in a church or the funeral home, followed by the gravesite burial and then what we all commonly called the wake which was essentially a party in honor of the departed. The wake could go on for hours and sometimes days depending on the individual who had passed on, their family and their status in the community. Regardless of the length of the wake there were two essential ingredients; music and alcohol. Some people would simply come and drink a shot of whiskey and move on while others would stay all night singing forlorn songs while rotating the bottle until they passed out.

As Margot, Deidre and I parked our car and rounded the corner to the Waterside Brewery we could tell that Annie's wake was well under way. The bar doors opened and a wave of music and voices chattering came flooding out to greet us as we entered the jam packed room. One of the local bands was playing a mariner's lullaby with a combination of fiddles, upright base, banjo and a woman's haunting songbird voice that spoke of finding eternal sleep. There were at least forty people gathered in front of the stage dancing in tight embraces, some exchanging feverish kisses affirming their life in the face of death. The tables were filled to capacity and it was standing room only at the bar as pitchers of brew were passed along in a line to all those who stood raising their glasses while shouting Annie's name.

Enveloped in the crowd it almost felt like being onboard a rocking ship where everyone swayed in time to the music in a lazy drift left to right and back again. It was only 4 p.m. and half the town was already too drunk to drive and there were children running under tables and up to the stage to get a closer look at the instruments. To an outsider it would have looked like a circus but to my insider's eye it was the image of a community moved to celebrate the life of one of their own and thumb their nose at death while doing it. The tears and the grieving had taken place, the bitterest traces of which were left on the sidewalks and buildings as Margot's lamentations had turned rain to snow. And now it was time to give Annie a proper send off into the afterlife with a tune and a drink.

As we made our way around the bar shaking hands and occasionally drinking a shot of whatever random glass of alcohol was handed to us I knew that it was not merely the living inhabitants of town that were taking part in the observances. In the balconies, tucked in the corners of the stage and some standing right in the middle of the dance floor were the many ghosts of Port Townsend. Tobias Gunn was followed closely by June and Hugo as he wove through the crowd toasting, yelping and limping with his bad leg. Several of the infamous prostitutes of the late 19th century sat atop the old piano watching the banjo player with languid eyes and slow motion movements. Young Pat Joss Jr., a former classmate of mine who had lost an arm in a logging accident and had bled out before he could be brought down from the cut site, was standing behind a table of his old colleagues and friends raising an imaginary glass with his one good arm. In and out they flickered waiting to see if Annie would join them in their revelry but I knew that she had already gone on to whatever was waiting in the light.

Margot stood rigid at the bar as Gavin leaned in to speak in her ear. The noise in the room drowned out any possibility for conversation. She nodded as he grabbed five wine glasses from behind the bar and motioned us to follow him into his office. We wove through the moving mass of people, some in tears and others gasping in frantic laughter. As Gavin opened the door to his office and we all slipped inside, the sudden quiet gave much relief with the muffled sounds of music just outside. Kat burst in behind us and threw herself into Margot arms with the unbridled spirit that was so innate to her.

"Oh Margot, I'm so sorry about Annie," she said with such feeling that even Margot had to smile and hug her back. We all sat at a round table that was in the center of the office where Gavin and Kat often gathered to taste new concoctions before making them available to the public. From high on a dust covered shelf Gavin reached up, tall enough to not need a ladder, and pulled down a familiar black bottle with a red wax seal. It was a bottle of Morgan's blackberry wine.

"I had been saving this for a special occasion and it just seemed like today was the right time to open this with all of us together." He pulled on the little red cord that removed the wax seal in one piece and then uncorked the bottle and began pouring the five of us a glass each. The dark liquid filled the room with a heady aroma of earth, blackberries and a hint of the smell of burning leaves. Raising his glass in the air Gavin said with his usual soft yet deep voice:

"To Annie," as we raised our own glasses and repeated in kind.

There we sat all together slowly drinking the blackberry wine. The rich flavor washed over our tongues and filled our bodies with a glowing warmth that had been absent since Morgan's reappearance and Annie's death. Waves of memories flooded through each of us as we reminisced about all the wild stories from Annie's youth and the quirkier moments of her old age. The rumble in the bar continued as people came and went. Several different bands took the stage to play a tune while the town sang along to everything from Elvis covers to the lesser known folk music of sailors lost at sea. We easily could have stayed there all night talking, drinking, crying and laughing but as the last drops of the bottle were swallowed down it was as if the clock had struck midnight and the spell for us was broken.

I glanced at the clock on Gavin's desk and it read 5:45 p.m. The sun would be going down soon and there was another ritual that we needed to attend to in order to save one of our own. Thanking Kat and Gavin the three of us gathered our things and made our way through the crowd one by one as not to attract attention to our leaving so early. Margot feigned fatigue when people asked where she was going and assured them that she would return later in the evening after taking a small nap. Deidre claimed she needed to check on Morgan at the hospital and that she too would return soon after. As I gave Kat and Gavin each a long hug I realized that it was odd that I hadn't seen Bee or Al.

"Have you seen Bee yet?" I asked since they hadn't been at the funeral either. Gavin leaned in trying not to shout in my ear as we were back in the middle of the packed bar.

"The bridge is closed because of all the snow, she called earlier," he said and I felt a mix of sadness and relief. If the bridge was closed than that meant James would not be able to get here until it was back open again which could be as soon as a few hours or as long as a few days. Whichever it would be it would buy me a little more time to hopefully complete the ritual and set things back into order.

"I still haven't found anything more linking Morgan to Father O'Malley," he said while leaning in again to all but shout in my ear. I had completely forgotten that I had asked him to help me decipher the clues of the past few days. I grabbed onto the lapel of his plaid shirt and pulled him closer to me so that the bystanders around us couldn't hear my words.

"Don't worry, I figured it all out. I promise I will tell you everything as soon as things are back in order." He gave me a startled and worried look. He knew when I was trying to be evasive. He pulled me close grabbing both of my arms while leaning in to speak to me in an annoyed tone.

"Hey, I know Charlotte speak," he said with a sudden furrowing of his brow. "What are you up to?"

"I can't talk about it here, Gavin. But I promise I will call you later tonight," I said in a hurried tone. Before he could say anything more I cut him off quickly with another request. "If James shows up tonight, take care of him ok?" I said, knowing that he and Kat would make him feel at home in this strange communion of souls celebrating life and death. Gavin loosened his grip and nodded a yes but his blue eyes pierced through me as he tried to divine what all I had discovered. I gave him a quick hug and rushed towards the door leaving him to fill pitchers of beer and random drinks for what would most likely be a very long evening. Moving through the mass of bodies I heard little snippets of people talking about Annie and even a few mentions of Elsiba. After pretending to have a headache, which wasn't hard to believe given the stitched gash on my forehead, I finally emerged back into the snow covered street. Margot and Deidre were standing by the car. The sun was just going down behind the mountains that rose up from the bay. For the first time in days the mist was clear and I could see the last of the light streaking across the sky as crepuscule descended on Port Townsend.

Without speaking we all got into the car and Deidre began to drive north. It was time to attempt the ritual to free Morgan's soul and hopefully escape unscathed in the process. The snow was still slick on the roads creating a glistening sheen in the fading light. While our car was heading north we could see headlights passing us in the opposite direction to give Annie her last respects. Winding down the road past the lagoon we each said a silent prayer as we passed both the cider mill and then Annie's house until the familiar sign up ahead signaled our turnoff. A weathered barn shingle pointed the way to what aged letters indicated was North Beach, the site of the ritual and the final resting place of Father O'Malley. As Deidre pulled into one of the empty parking spots that sat above the vast expanse of ocean and sand we all sat for a moment. With our energy gathered to us we finally stepped out into the fast approaching night to commence the exorcism and binding of the demon Malphus.

CHAPTER 34

The peculiar smell of ocean air had always been something that reminded me of home in a way that felt mysteriously irresistible. Tonight the crashing waves and crisp cold air carried with it the perfect mix of salt and seaweed intertwined to create the oddest of perfumes. Looking out over the vast ocean with the light fading fast from the sky I scanned for the perfect spot to start the bonfire and begin the ritual. Deidre had brought dry kindling and while everything on the grassy dunes was covered in snow the beach had been washed clean by the last tide.

Carefully we helped Margot down the sandy path that led to the beach below and immediately I knew the spot where Father O'Malley had left his clothing before giving himself to the frigid waters. A ghostly outline of their remnants remained like an imprint that my eyes alone could see. Quickly Deidre began to stack the wood into a teepee shape and stuff the newspaper in-between the kindling we had brought with us to get the fire blazing. I dragged over dry driftwood that had been sheltered beneath larger logs to add to the flames in order to keep the fire burning long into the night. The fire began to blaze just as the last bit of light faded from the sky. All that was left were dark outlines of the surrounding trees on one side and the black nothingness of ocean on the other. On the drive over my stomach had been bound up in knots with an impending sense of doom. Now that I was preparing to begin the ritual, a wave of calm washed over me as my mind became focused and alert.

Anyone who has spent time near the ocean knows that you never turn your back to it regardless of how calm the water may seem. A rogue wave can sneak up on you as fast as a snake and drag you into the under-tow where up feels like down and all light is lost. So with the fire between us Margot, Deidre and I spread out to form a triangle with myself facing the water and the two of them on either side only half turned so as to always have an eye out for large waves. The fire was blazing into a perfect point and gave the few wind swept trees on the shore an almost life-like shadow. Their tortured outstretched arms reached towards us as I began the ritual that was Morgan's last hope of survival.

Each of us began to call on their own element as guardians; I could feel my feet rooting into the earth like the same trees that stood curiously watching nearby. My body was solid and strong with the connection to the ground beneath me and all the living creatures that were earth bound as well. Margot tilted her head back while spreading her arms out to her sides and called on the rain to keep us from harm by fire. Light drops of rain began to fall and the waves crashed louder around us as her element was beckoned to her. Deidre called to the air and the birds to be our protectors and in an immediate response the sky was filled with owls, eagles and ravens all flocking to the nearby trees to watch over us.

Finally as one we began to call Malphus by all his names commanding him to show himself to the blood that ran through his host's veins. At first there was only a persistent silence that seemed to mock our efforts. We continued to thrust all our energy together into the fire before us to summon the demon from Morgan in the hopes that it would show itself on this cursed shore. The waves began to crash more furiously as Margot's frustration increased. I could feel the owls' stares fixated on the strange spectacle of our ritual. Then in the distance we began to hear what sounded like screeching coming from above the forest line from the direction of where the hospital stood.

Before I knew what was happening the sky above us darkened to a pitch black of flapping wings as thousands of crows filled the night sky. Unlike the ravens that were waiting as our sentinels on the shore these creatures were not made of normal flesh and blood. This was the demon broken into a thousand evil parts. The crows began to dive from the sky heading directly for us. As one was about to peck at Margot's eyes a huge barn owl swooped in and with talon claws tore into the wicked bird. The skies around us were filled with the horrid sounds of Deidre's birds battling Malphus' crows. We continued to chant with increasing ferocity the words that Elsiba had whispered to me in sleep.

The fire was now blazing to new heights as we demanded that Malphus be bound back into the flames from which it came and release its mortal host for all eternity. The ground beneath us began to shudder as our combined concentration was being pushed to the brink with the noise of owls, eagles and ravens being slaughtered on all sides. The rain was pounding heavily upon the beach protecting our bodies from the flames. In the melee I could hear Deidre's chant interspersed with hysterical sobs as the bodies of her beloved winged creatures were falling all around her dead.

With each passing second I could hear that the night birds in all their devotion to us were still losing out to the crows. Little by little the sounds of their cries became less and less in contrast to the rasping screeches of Malphus's familiars. Soon it was just the crows hovering above us. All of our warrior birds had fallen into heaps of scattered carnage and featherless carcasses stretching the length of the deserted beach.

With doubled energy our three voices grew louder as our minds became frantic with fear. Margot raised her voice above all of us unleashing a crack of lighting that lit the sky overhead. It was followed by a thunderous boom that made my heart skip a beat. Instantly the bolt of lightning transferred from the open sky into our outstretched hands creating a perfect triangle between us. The current of energy linking us together kept the crows overhead at bay and created an arc of light. In this moment a connection was created between us and with it our thoughts become one.

Margot called on the water to pour down and wash the crows from our midst and with another crack of lighting the sky opened up to unleash a torrent of rain. The huge drops scattered the flocks from above while melting all the accumulated snow and ice. Again we concentrated our efforts and demanded that Malphus leave Morgan's being and make itself known to us in the fire. The electric connection that was blazing from our hands uniting us was like a streak of vibrant blue holding the red flames of the bonfire at its center. In one voice we began to scream over the sounds of pouring rain, crashing waves and increasingly violent winds that Malphus would obey our commands.

It was in a rush of wings that Malphus appeared as all the

crows funneled into the bonfire flames. The pyre transformed into an immense pillar of fire that rose to sky scraper heights before us. We tried to hold on to the current but the flames were too much for the three of us to keep contained. With a violent burst we were all blown backwards severing the electric connection between us. I saw Deidre crumble to the ground. Margot was flung through the air like a rag doll landing hard on a pile of sharp rocks. I was thrust onto the sand and moved just in time to avoid a huge piece of drift wood from tumbling onto me.

The fire blazed like a beacon of torment reaching well over a hundred feet into the air. It held at its center a multitude of bodies writhing in pain. These were the souls that Malphus had claimed leading up to Morgan over the millennia of abuse and manipulation it had enjoyed. I tried to run to Margot but was blown back into the sand by the power of the flames. I could see what looked like a pool of blood beginning to form under the side of her head. There was a small line of red trickling from her mouth and her eyes were closed although I could not tell if she was breathing. On my knees I started to crawl towards Deidre who was slowly stirring. Again I was blown back across the sand as if I was nothing more than an ant being brushed off of a table top.

As I peered up into the flames a sudden sense of defeat filled my body. Falling onto my back in the wet sand surrounded by thousands of dead birds my heart was overcome with such despair that I could hardly move my limbs. I had failed Morgan and now our fate was in the hands of this demon that we had foolishly summoned convinced that we were stronger than it. All I could think was that Elsiba had been wrong to put her faith into me and now Margot could very well be mortally injured and Deidre had lost all her dearest creatures. All of this lost for nothing more than our own hubris in the face of a God. Morgan would still be cursed to waste away and the Winship line would end once and for all with me on this destitute beach.

These thoughts persisted as the flames grew higher still lighting the sand with horrible orange and red shadows. The fire flickered and shot out to lick our hands and feet as the base of the flames expanded. Turning my head to once again find Margot I was met with the sight of her blood spilling into an expanding dark pool beneath her. Her eyes were still closed as if in a deep sleep. I then turned to the other side to find Deidre. Her eyes locked on mine as she again struggled to stand. In my mind I heard her words ring through my ears like a bell.

"Don't let it talk to you." Her voice echoed through the growing despair. "It is time, call them to us. Call 'the Strangers,' NOW!"

With the last of my energy I struggled to my knees, lifted my head up to the sky and with every last drop of hope implored the heavens with these words:

"If you are beings of light, sent to us by Morgan to rid us of the affliction that is before us I beseech you to come to us now in our time of need. Mal'ak come to us through air, through earth, through water and through fire to bind the demon Malphus from causing harm to any living creature. If you are beings of light than we are your servants until the end of days and we beg you to come to us NOW! "

I fell back into the sand, emptied of the last of my energy. The flames continued to rise mocking our attempts to defeat it. Deidre was sobbing and Margot still lay motionless on the jagged rocks. Just when it seemed that all was lost I thought that I noticed two figures approaching across the water before my eyes closed letting the world turn black.

CHAPTER 35

Somewhere on the other side of consciousness I could hear the chaos on the beach drift closer. I must have blacked out for only a few minutes because when my eyes fluttered open again I could clearly see "the Strangers" walking on the water towards us. They moved slowly in a straight line, instep and still dressed in their black clothes and Stetson hats. I struggled to sit up. Margot was still motionless although Deidre was on her feet again staring into the immense tunnel of fire before her. I managed to rise to my knees although my entire body was filled with searing pain. As I looked out to the rolling waves that were bringing "the Strangers" closer to us I began to feel an unexpected burst of hope.

They halted at the water's edge. With a simultaneous clap of their hands that echoed off the cliffs and drowned out all sound Margot began to stir. She slowly rose to her feet, pushing her crumpled body to stand upright again regardless of the massive pool of blood that had seeped from her body into the sand. Her eyes shot to mine and then Deidre. With renewed strength emanating from her body she raised her arms, ready again to fight the entity. The blue current of electricity reappeared between us connected our perfect triangle of light. This time we all felt an indestructible force rise between us. Despite the constant strain of Malphus surging against us we held strong. Margot's voice rang out across the desolate beach with stunning power.

"I call on the beings of light to aid us in the binding of this demon, Malphus, and in doing so send it back into the void from which it came releasing Morgan and all others from its power," she said as Deidre and I joined in to repeat the words that were intended to release Morgan and banish the demon. With each syllable Malphus pushed back with flames filled with the images of contorted faces in the fire. This time we held fast as we heard another thunderous clap resonate from "the Strangers" hands.

Still at the water's edge the second clap created a small whirlpool just off the shore. The swirling black waters spiraled faster and faster until up out of the center the body of Father John O'Malley began to emerge. At first all that was left was a skeleton picked clean of its flesh. It was all that was left after years of being abandoned on the ocean floor. Like seaweed sliding over the bleached white bones the skeleton began to regain exposed muscle. Skin soon followed and within moments the skeleton emerged as the clothed figure of Father O'Malley. He was exactly as I had seen him in ghostly form but now made whole again. He walked across the water joining "the Strangers" and while I could see Margot flinch when she saw him moving towards us it was now clear that they were our unexpected allies.

Together they moved across the beach until each of "the Strangers" was standing to either side of me while Father O'Malley was opposite with his back to the ocean. Keeping our triangle of energy streaming between us took a tremendous amount of focus. It took all my effort not to black out again as the clothing slipped from "the Strangers" bodies, revealing what lay beneath their earthly disguise. Their bodies from the waist down were covered with brilliant orange and red scales like a magnificent serpent made with rubies and bits of the sun. They grew even brighter as they slowly unfolded six immense fiery wings that made Malphus' once impressive blaze look pale by comparison. The light from their bodies was almost blinding and as I shot a look to Margot I could hear her whisper in my mind "these are the Seraphim."

Then it came to me in a flash, all those years ago when I had been but a small child and Margot held me in her arms telling me the stories of the many angels that made up the heavens. The Seraphim were the closest to God and guarded his throne. It had always frightened me as a child that they were described as looking like dragons or snakes. I preferred the images of the Guardian angels who looked like lovely Victorian ladies in flowing robes with kind faces to the image of snake-like creatures. But Margot had always insisted that just because something may seem menacing at first that did not mean that it meant harm. The word Seraphim meant "the fiery ones," as they were inflamed with their passion for God and all things that presided on earth. They were also the keepers of human history and I couldn't help but wonder if they were here not only because Morgan had summoned them but also to keep the Winship history, as small as it was in the scheme of things, alive a bit longer.

As Margot, Deidre and I struggled to keep our blue current flowing from our bodies, holding Malphus inside its lines, the Seraphim and Father O'Malley raised their arms to unleash a fiery stream of light from their hands creating a second triangle. Their blazing orange triangle sat directly on top of ours and together they made a perfect six pointed star with the tunnel of flames shuddering at its center. A horrific scream shot forth from Malphus as Father O'Malley used his voice to chant for the three of them commanding the demon to leave Morgan Winship's body and return to oblivion bound from harming any soul. The blue and orange fiery star began to shoot flaming cords around Malphus essentially fighting fire with fire as Elsiba had said half a century earlier. Then with one final spasm the fire that was Malphus collapsed in on itself leaving only a tiny floating globe of flames hovering in the center of our star.

With another loud clap of their hands the Seraphim broke the connection of the star while the fiery globe that now contained the entity dissolved into a pile of black ash on the sand. A quiet descended on the ravaged beach as Margot, Deidre and I ran into each other's arms inspecting Margot's now non-existent wound while gasping for breath and hanging on to each other in order to stay standing. After a moment of swooning we slowly turned to face the Seraphim and Father O'Malley, feeling tremendous relief that Malphus was gone forever. The Seraphim had returned to wearing their earthly disguises of dark suits and Stetson hats which made it much easier to look directly at them. Father O'Malley stood between them head bowed staring at the sand. The sky was oddly lit up in a saturated purple hue that added to the forlorn expression on Father O'Malley's face. Silently Margot approached the three of them walking confidently across the wet sand with little violet stars of light radiating from her body. Standing directly in front of Father O'Malley she straightened her frail back to her tallest and with a calm voice she said:

"Father John O'Malley, I forgive you."

He looked up into her eyes and nodded silently. His one expression of humble gratitude was evidenced in the flow of tears that began to stream down his face. Bit by bit little pieces of his newly reformed skin began to detach and float up into the sky twisting on the invisible breath of wind that carried them. With increasing speed his body began to disintegrate as each piece of skin transformed into a tiny fluttering brown and blue moth. They swirled up into a spiral of papery wings until he was gone; finally free of the evil that had inhabited him and no longer a weary spirit riddled with guilt.

Margot raised her hands together in a symbol of prayer and bent herself to both the Seraphim in a formal bow of thanks and honor. As she made her way back to us Deidre dropped to her knees, with sudden exhaustion, to cradle the broken body of a white snow owl in her arms. She began to sob while whispering under her breath "my poor friends" with so much sorrow that my heart felt like it would break along with hers. While I wanted to drop down beside her and comfort her I felt frozen in place. I could not seem to take my eyes off the Seraphim and in my mind I thanked them with the only ill adapted words I had in my human vocabulary.

Motionless they simply nodded in response and with a final clap of their hands they performed one last miracle as all the birds that littered the beach and surrounding forest sprung suddenly back to life. Deidre screamed as the white snow owl fluttered in her hands equally surprised to once again be alive. A vibrant commotion of wings and sudden life filled the beach where there had once been so much death and destruction. In the midst of the resurrected birds the Seraphim were suddenly gone having fulfilled their purpose with grace and divinity.

Deidre and I let out screams of joy and began spinning around in the sand like children unable to control our relief until we noticed Margot sitting silently on a nearby rock. Rushing to her side we realized that in our burst of happiness at having bound Malphus we had begun our victory celebration far too soon. Without speaking we rushed back to the car as the rain began to fall again hard on the beach sending the birds back to their nests as we rushed to the hospital. Had our binding of the demon set Morgan free or had it been the final straw that would end his already fragile life with one swift blow? We would soon find out.

CHAPTER 36

The distance between North Beach and the hospital passed in what seemed like a slow motion blur of pouring rain, flapping wings and tense silence. We knew that Malphus was no longer in existence but until we reached the hospital we had no way to know if Morgan had survived the removal of the entity or if he was lost to us. Margot had her head bent in concentration as Deidre sped through stop signs, her hands tightly clasping the steering wheel. After what felt like an eternity we sped into the empty parking lot and all three of us ran through the deluge of water that was thrashing the pavement and washing every last piece of snow from the ground.

Down the familiar hallway we rushed and turned the corner to see Samir frantically struggling to open the door to Morgan's room. It was locked from the inside. As we threw ourselves up against the viewing window we were met by a horrific sight. Unable to decipher exactly what we were seeing we all stood mute while Samir continued to struggle with the door in vain.

"It started about fifteen minutes ago," said Samir in a voice riddled with panic. "The door is locked from the inside!"

Through the viewing window we could see Morgan writhing and convulsing on the hospital bed in the cold white room. His body was twisting itself into improbable positions while his skin undulated. With eyes rolled back in his head, he began to scream wildly as his skin cracked like the shell on a hard-boiled egg. The scale-like burns were moving in waves over his body and slowly it began to peel back; cracking and tearing with each contortion. The first layer of skin to come off was on his hands. He grasped madly at the burnt flakes in order to tear and rip until a new layer appeared beneath it. Frantically he scratched and pulled as if trying to wiggle himself out of the old epidermis that had imprisoned him for days. He was now standing with his back to us as his spine rippled. With a grotesque ripping noise the skin surrounding it tore in one long line as he shrugged off the husk that had enclosed him. The last piece to go was the skin on his face. He turned towards the observation window and with both hands pulled back the deformed mask that had left him nearly unrecognizable.

Margot gasped as underneath was a perfect new skin, milky white and without blemish. He opened his black eyes which were again both visible and unharmed. Staring directly at the three of us all sign of confusion began to clear from his eyes. We heard the door lock click open allowing Samir to go crashing in. Margot and Deidre rushed in behind Samir and they all began to free Morgan of the cursed skin revealing a man reborn from the ashes. I stood frozen outside the window in a state of complete shock at the realization that Morgan was now truly free. For the first time there was no black shadow hovering nor was there the smell of burnt hair and leaves but instead a feeling of tremendous power and light came rushing from the room. The creeping demons in the hallways scurried away to hide from this man that was shining as brightly as a lone star at sea.

In that moment our eyes met through the glass and he understood all that had taken place since he had been in the coma. A rush of knowledge passed between us in a flash of images without spoken words. He simply nodded in thanks and then closed his eyes as the others continued to work to free him completely from his burnt cage. I carefully made my way into the room not wanting to be too close for fear of disturbing their efforts but also intimidated by the waves of power that were emanating from Morgan. I had always known that he was a force to be reckoned with but it was only now without the constraints of the demon that his real power was free. As Deidre tore a piece of skin from his shoulder I noticed that the star mark he was born with was now gone and beneath it only pure new skin.

It took almost an hour for him to completely shed his old skin. I sat helpless in a chair as Samir, Deidre and Margot worked away on his body. He eventually laid himself back down in the hospital bed when they finished removing the last pieces and I could tell that he was thoroughly exhausted. It took another two hours for Samir to convince the burn specialist that Morgan should be released to go home with us.

Needless to say the doctor was speechless and visibly shaken to see all the damaged skin littering the floor of the hospital room and Morgan completely unharmed. He kept muttering that it wasn't possible and nervously cleaned his eye glasses as if the spectacles were to blame for the sight that was before him. From this moment on Morgan was to shed his old town nickname of "Dr. Doom" to a new one of "Snake Man" although he never really paid the town much attention. The burn specialist simply refused to believe what he had seen and was convinced that the whole thing had been some type of hoax when questioned about it later. Eventually he gave in and signed the release forms while Samir rustled up a pair of scrubs and an old pair of his sneakers so Morgan could leave with us and return home.

Walking out of the hospital the few people who were not at Annie's wake hovered in the hallways whispering about how Morgan was really half snake and how they always knew something was not right with him. I could already imagine the tales that would be spun in the years to come about the "Snake Man" but for now I simply felt a sense of relief and fatigue that combined left me slightly numb. Morgan walked slowly with one arm around Samir and the other around Deidre as Margot and I rushed ahead to open the car door. The rain was still pouring in torrents and if it kept up there would certainly be flooding by the morning.

As we all walked in the door of the Winship house the Grandfather clock on the second floor began to bong twelve loud times signaling that it was midnight. There was a rustle of wings outside as the night birds continued to follow us like feathered guardians protecting their own. Slowly Samir helped Morgan up to his old bedroom where Margot turned down his bed and helped him into the familiar blankets of his childhood. As she loaded the small wood stove with fresh logs in the corner of his room preparing to light it and take the chill out of the air Morgan simply waved his hand and a flame burst forth creating a well contained fire. I gasped as I realized how much control he now had over his gift. Before it had always turned on him but now it seemed that it was effortless. My gasp alerted his attention and he gave me a wry smile before settling into his space and closing his eyes for what would surely be a long night's repose.

Silently we all made our way to the kitchen. As Margot and Deidre told Samir all that had happened I noticed a little blinking light on the rarely used answering machine. Pressing the play button Bee's voice sounded on the recording:

"Hello, this is Bee. The bridge is closed so we couldn't make it over for the wake but it was just as well because a bee came in the house this morning which means a visitor was on their way. And low and behold Charlotte's young man James was stuck here in Port Gamble because of all the weather business. So he is staying with us tonight and will be coming over with us in the morning when the bridge should be right as rain again. See you in the morning and sweet dreams."

I felt a sudden lightheaded feeling come over me as I sank into my chair at the table. If James was staying with Bee then he would be getting the full story on our strange family straight from her with none of my careful editing. I had wanted to ease him in to things but it seemed that fate had other plans. Now all I could do was hope that Bee hadn't scared him off already before I could explain the family and our gifts. I felt a wave of panic come over me and tears began to threaten as I excused myself before anyone could notice and climbed the three flights up to my turret room. I flopped onto my bed and gave in to indulgent sobs as the intensity of the night washed out of me like the continuing rain fall outside my window.

The images played back and forth in my mind of all that had transpired in such a short amount of time. It still felt like it had all been some sort of twisted dream. Morgan was home safe, the entity Malphus was gone, "the Strangers" had been the key all along and Father O'Malley was finally at rest. These things should have left me feeling elated but instead I felt a selfish worry that made my throat tighten with tears in that I now had to finally face what I truly was once and for all. I was a Winship and I could no longer deny it.

I picked up the phone and dialed the Waterside Brewery. Not only did I owe it to Gavin to tell him all that had happened tonight but I also needed to hear a reassuring voice. I let it ring over ten times before he finally picked up. There was a woman singing in the background in a siren's mourning wail. The hum of people still lamenting Annie's death was so loud he told me to wait until he could get into his office.

"What the hell, Charlotte?" was the first thing that came out of his mouth as I heard the door shut on the line, cutting off the noise from the bar. I was feeling so fragile that I almost burst into tears again.

"Morgan is home with us, Gavin," I said, swallowing hard as I told him all that had happened from the time I had left the bar. I could imagine his jaw hanging open the whole time on the other line. When I finished all was silent for a moment and I wondered if he hadn't dropped the phone somewhere mid-explanation.

"I missed the fireworks," was what he finally said with such childlike disappointment that I let out an unexpected laugh. There had been a demon, two angels and a monk ghost all wrapped into one curse and somehow he took it all in and believed every word that I said. We went over the details and slowly my heart began to lighten.

"James is staying with Bee and Al tonight because of the bridge being down," I said, hoping he would get my meaning. He did. Gavin and James got along well but he knew that I still hadn't told him about myself or my family.

"With Bee, huh," he said in a contemplative voice, "don't worry, Charlotte. If James is as good of a guy as I think he is then he will be more intrigued than frightened away. Whatever happens, you won't know unless you let him in on all the juicy stuff."

"Well that is another way of putting it," I snorted, "juicy ghost gossip."

"Way more interesting than your usual cocktail party conversation," he said. With each jest my heart felt a bit lighter. I was still exhausted and nervous but I felt less despair than I had only a half hour before. When we finally hung up, he told me to come by the bar with James in the morning as the wake would most likely still be underway. I promised him I would and hung up feeling relieved that at least my best friend had been privy to all the strange happenings of the past few days.

One by one I heard everyone climb the stairs below to their rooms to dream of Annie and all the beautiful things that had been her life coupled with relief that Morgan was safe once again. Eventually I cried myself to sleep out of fatigue and worry with the familiar comforting presence of Fox hovering in the corner of the room. When the clock struck three am I could almost hear the house sigh with contentment that all the Winships were safe within its walls once again.

CHAPTER 37

The sunshine blazing in through the windows of my room are what woke me up the next morning. I groggily realized the rain that had eventually lulled me to sleep the night before had finally given way to light. Peeking out the window it was a shock to see that all the snow was gone as if it had been merely a figment of my imagination. Still struggling with sleep I began to wonder if all of this week's events had been some sort of hallucination until I reached my hand up and felt the stitches on my head and acknowledged that every part of my body ached.

Robins were picking at the grass searching for insects that had been well hidden under the snowfall and the rays of yellow gold created new shadows on the walls and floor of my turret room. Slowly I dressed and began to make my way downstairs in search of large doses of both coffee and aspirin. Nothing seemed to stir as I heard the familiar snores of Samir coming down the hall on the second floor as I reached the landing and noted that Margot's door was still closed. Just as I was about to continue down to the kitchen a flash of rainbow light flickered from the open door of the Winship library.

Quietly tiptoeing down the hall as not to disturb anyone I turned the corner into the library expecting it to be empty and instead found Morgan sitting at the old table. He was dressed in his usual attire of black jeans and a black sweater, hair slightly askew and his notebook that I had found only a few days before in his long thin hands. I stood perfectly still in the doorway not knowing how to announce my entrance. I had the overwhelming feeling of being a small child in the presence of the power that radiated from him. Without raising his eyes from the book he spoke in his usual deadpan tone:

"I don't know how she can sleep next to that noise," he said. "Maybe she's in a coma?" Then he flashed one of his wry grins at me. I shyly smiled back and took his humor to be an invitation to come inside.

"I found it a few days ago. I'm sorry I couldn't figure it all out faster," I said while pulling out the chair across from him.

"It takes the time that it takes," he responded as another rainbow light flickered through the room and left a reflection on the left side of his face. I glanced around looking for something made of crystal that was catching the sunbeams but could find nothing. I had a million questions running through my mind but I could not seem to put them into any order that would make sense. Finally the one thing that didn't seem to fit popped into my head:

"Why were the ghosts so fearful of the Seraphim?" I said as I remembered back to those first moments when "the Strangers" felt like a menace and the reactions of the town ghosts were highly unusual. He closed his notebook and set it lightly on the table and then, measuring his words, replied:

"Your element is earth Charlotte and that is why the earthbound things speak to you in a way they cannot with others; you know this. The Seraphim are pure angelic light and fire or what most people refer to as the light at the end of tunnel or a dozen other metaphors for leaving this earth and going to another reality. The ghosts that have stayed behind fear the light because they cannot let go of whatever it is that is holding them to this earth. Either for reasons of violent sudden death, unfinished business, regret or simple fear of the unknown they remain bound here until the light comes for them whether they like it or not. Or they are able to resolve whatever wrong they feel they have done, or has been done to them, and eventually go to the light willingly."

He sat staring at me waiting for me to acknowledge my comprehension. As his words swirled in my mind it all clicked together and finally made sense except for one thing.

"They came to Annie," I said with my voice suddenly cracking "and she died the next day. Was she the payment for binding Malphus?"

Before I could register what was happening Morgan was doubled over with what looked like pain and then I realized that he was laughing. At me.

"No," he said with a sarcastic lilt to his voice and I suddenly felt like the most dimwitted member of the family. "The light requires no payment. It was just Annie's time and they escorted her home. The only things that take in order to give something back are the dark entities or the ones that try to use their power to better themselves. It is a vicious circle and one that I have struggled with for a very long time. Until today that is," he smiled and again the rainbows flashed across the room twinkling in the ever growing brightness that was pouring through the windows of the Winship house.

"Where were you all those years?" I asked fearing the answer and assuming he would brush me off or clam up. Morgan had always been secretive about his comings and goings from town and since he had left without ever sending word I assumed that he wanted it to remain a mystery.

"I tried to follow the footsteps backwards to where the monk first became possessed by the entity," he said and I noticed that he did not use the entity's name. I sat quietly hoping he would go on and eventually he continued in a soft far off voice as if he was picturing in his mind the long journey he had been on.

"I headed south first to San Francisco where I found the mother house where he had lived for a time until the possession had left the order no choice but to find a way to exorcise him. This was why he had come here to Father Benedict for help. The other priests had complained about his odd behavior and his obsessions with various women that they were sure would have a devious end. I would listen carefully as the entity inside of me would slowly give away clues as it tried to manipulate me with half-truths. In the end I found the spot where the entity had first taken hold." He paused and I was almost on the edge of my seat hoping he would continue.

"It was in the Mohave desert where Father O'Malley was first possessed. In his piety and naiveté he decided to go out to that vast expanse of sand and tortured trees to spend forty days and forty nights fasting as Jesus had in the Judean desert. I think in some way he hoped that the devil would come to him and that he would spite him and be found that much more beautiful in the eyes of God. In the end I don't know if it was his pride that eventually opened the doors to the entity or possibly the fact that deep down he didn't really believe that such things existed. Whatever it was he did not walk out of that desert alone and from that moment on the darkness began to devour him."

We sat in silence for a moment as I imaged Father O'Malley walking through the Joshua trees and in between the rocks as the sun set and the night creatures began to emerge from their hiding places in the abandoned sands. Then I could see Morgan walking the same path and I shuddered at the thought of him alone for all those years searching for a way to be free of the curse that had bound him since birth.

"How did you get back here?" I said as I could again hear Margot's words only a few days before describing how Morgan's body was found in the hospital parking lot burnt and near death. To see him sitting here before me restored and glowing with power and light was dizzying.

"It's complicated," he said with another of his wry smiles. "I tried the ritual in the desert alone calling on the elements and asking the Seraphim to burn the entity from me. The heat was too much and as the entity fought it called on its own dark allies to finish me off. In my last attempt to save myself I willed myself home." He stopped for a moment but I could tell that he wasn't finished but was rather struggling to find the right words. "Time and space are malleable but it is not without risk. With my last bit of life and energy I called the Seraphim again as I laid in the hospital parking lot so very close to home yet completely broken."

"You sent me the raven in my dream, didn't you?" I asked as everything began to finally make perfect sense.

"I did. And the dark creatures tried their best to keep you and the Seraphim from uniting here." I could see that he was starting to become weary again and had to remind myself that just last night he had been in a coma and burnt over ninety percent of his body.

We sat in silence as the sun beamed into the room and the rainbow reflections continued to dance across our skin playfully.

"What will you do now?" I finally asked. He thought about it for a minute before responding.

"I think I will rebuild my house first and see where things lead after that."

Outside the window a series of muffled car doors opening and slamming shut echoed into the room. Morgan looked wistfully towards the willow tree that was brushing against the old glass of the bay windows and without getting up from his chair he looked at me and said:

"I think you have a visitor."

I stood feeling a nervous rush come over me as I knew that James was probably making his way to the front door with Bee and Al. My face flushed red as I was both filled with joy at the thought of seeing the man that I loved as well as terror that he would think we were all a bunch of freaks only to run screaming out of town. On wobbly legs I made my way to the hall and I thought I heard Morgan mumble under his breath:

"I hope for your sake he doesn't snore," with his usual sarcastic tone.

As I reached the bottom of the stairs I noticed Bee's familiar shape on the other side of the stained glass that made up the front door of the Winship house. I hopped down the last few steps and opened the door to see Bee and Al smiling at me. They ushered themselves past after giving me ample hugs and then continued into the kitchen as Bee proclaimed that she would get the coffee started.

There on the long walkway that lead up to the house stood James. He had a dreamy look on his face as he peered up to my turret room transfixed by the conical roof and the delicate shingles that scalloped along its edge. The sun was shining brightly on him lighting his face with a perfect halo making him handsome with his childlike expression of wonder. As I stepped onto the covered porch and took in the sight of him here in my home, so many miles from everything that he knew or had ever imagined, I was filled with joy.

As he noticed me standing there his lips immediately curled into a huge grin as his eyes twinkled with the same glint that had appeared the first time we met.

"It's beautiful," he said almost with a gasp as he pointed at the house that embodied everything that it meant to be a Winship. I skipped down the stairs and into his arms. I lingered in his embrace long enough to take in the smell of green leaves that arose from his skin. Then taking his hand I began to pull him after me into the garden.

"Let me know show you the willow tree," I said as we walked into the sunshine with him stumbling behind me as he tried to examine every archway and twisted finial. I knew from this moment on there would never be any more secrets between us.

ACKNOWLEDGEMENTS

Embarking on the writing of the Winship stories has been an amazing experience that started on a quick trip to my childhood home of Port Townsend with a dear group of musician friends. Thank you to Antonette Goroch Bevelacqua, Michelle Kappel-Stone and Matty Stone for planting the seed and encouraging it to take root on that trip. The Cupcake Diaries Tour will forever be the moment I started writing again after so many years of hibernation.

I must also thank my family that has passed on to other side. My Grandparents who bravely pushed west and made a home on Willow Street for over fifty years of marriage. My Grandmother always encouraged the creativity in her loved ones and would have been thrilled at the thought of my writing a book. My Grandfather who took me kite flying on windy days and inspired all things whimsical. And for my uncle who is at the center of this story. Beneath his struggles with light and dark there was a brilliant mind I wish I could have known better.

Now for the living! I have many thanks to give to my first readers who pushed me to keep writing into the wee hours of the night. To Laura Carriker I am forever grateful for the continued enthusiasm for the Winships. It was her undying curiosity for their adventures that have kept me pushing forward. To Antonette (Mom) and Alexandra Goroch for always being the loving voices of encouragement and praise whenever my doubts arose. You are my soul sisters. To Jeanne-Marie Ramsey for taking the time to read my book twice: once as my loving friend and a second time as my copy editor extraordinaire. To Leta Rose Scott for all her tireless work in making sure the light always prevails in my life and my work. There is no one I trust more with the layers of these stories than you dear friend. To Wendy Moss Thomas for her continued friendship and support of all things creative and beautiful! Our girl's nights out fuel the creative fires. Many thanks to Megan Thornley for reading as fast as I could write the chapters and always exchanging her own stories in return. Fellow writers till the end! And I give my everlasting gratitude to Emily Morrison and Jennifer Elizabeth Jahahn for being my witchy sisters who believe in all things magical.

Most of all I want to thank my family. For my Mom who bravely raised me to embrace art and life despite the odds against us. It is her belief in our dreams transforming into reality and for her own creative heart and spirit taking flight in painting that push me to create. For my Dad who had the more difficult job of insisting I focus on all things practical in addition to my desires to be an artist. The two combined are the magical component to make things emerge into being.

And to my husband who has been by my side for well over a decade always encouraging my love of all things creative. If not for his eye at detecting the fatal flaws in the story and for offering his help with all things technological the book may have remained a mere idea. His insistence that we could put it into the world ourselves has given me the courage to keep pushing forward with the Winships. I thank him for his love and for his ability to share me with the many late nights I am up writing the imaginary world of my characters.

Also huge thanks to the town of Port Townsend for remaining a constant inspiration for my work. I hope the residents will please forgive me for switching up all kinds of names and places for the purpose of fiction. To Tom Camfield for his amazing books on the history of the region although again I apologize for scrambling dates to fit into my own story. My "Crow's Nest" at the Palace Hotel is ideal for late night writing and perfect Victorian ambiance, besides Grandma's house, there is no other spot that feels so much like home. Also a thank you to all of the friends and family that I have not mentioned but who are very much the reason this book has come forth.

Spring has come unnaturally early to the shores of Port Townsend. Only two weeks before her daughter's sixteenth birthday, Charlotte Winship is visited by the ghosts of children who died of a strange fever nearly one hundred years to the date. These spirits warn of a coming plague that fuels her to piece together the tragic events of the past in order to keep both her family and the town from grave harm. Charlotte, now a wife and mother of two, follows the ghosts to unearth the mysteries of old in order to keep them from repeating in her beloved town. With the Winship family at her side, Charlotte is faced with overcoming the most insidious of creatures; the vampire.

Made in the USA
Charleston, SC
26 January 2013